Party Games

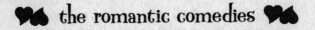
the romantic comedies

Party Games

WHITNEY LYLES

Simon Pulse
New York London Toronto Sydney

This book is a work of fiction. Any references to historical events, real people, or real locales are used fictitiously. Other names, characters, places, and incidents are the product of the author's imagination, and any resemblance to actual events or locales or persons, living or dead, is entirely coincidental.

SIMON PULSE
An imprint of Simon & Schuster Children's Publishing Division
1230 Avenue of the Americas, New York, NY 10020
Copyright © 2008 by Whitney Lyles
All rights reserved, including the right of reproduction in whole or in part in any form.
SIMON PULSE and colophon are registered trademarks of Simon & Schuster, Inc.
Designed by Ann Zeak
The text of this book was set in Garamond 3.
Manufactured in the United States of America
First Simon Pulse edition June 2008
10 9 8 7 6 5 4 3 2 1
Library of Congress Control Number 2008922274
ISBN-13: 978-1-4169-5913-7
ISBN-10: 1-4169-5913-0

#4.99 8/12

For Jennifer and Chip

Acknowledgments

Huge thanks to my wonderful agent, Elise Capron, for all her priceless advice, hard work, and continuous support. Looking forward to many more growth spurts in the future.

I am forever indebted to my brilliant editor, Sangeeta Mehta. Not only a wise guide, she has been a true champion for this book. Thanks for all the sharp feedback, and for helping shape the book into what it is today. Thanks to everyone else at Simon Pulse, especially Katherine Devendorf and Sandra Smith for all the fine-tuning with this book.

Many thanks to the SDLA team for all their hard work, especially Sandy Dijkstra, Taryn Fagerness, Kelly Sonnack, and Elisabeth James.

As always, thanks to my husband, Rob Dodds, who stepped up to the plate as Mr. Mom during the final crunch of my deadline, and to Charlotte for being such a good girl.

Thanks to Hollie Gieselmann for all her support and for providing great answers to all my dumb questions.

Thanks to Mom, Dad, Carol, Doug, Chip, Liz, Veeve, Del, Sophie, Annie, Rev. Jim Williams, Liz Harris, Tara Geier, Agatha Miller, Kelly Towne, Amy Kaechele, Mike Sirota, and all friends and family who continue to cheer for me.

One

The energy in the reception hall felt charged. Dance floor in full bloom, the buzz of conversation hummed against lively music. Waiters in black ties darted throughout the ballroom, balancing trays spiked with bubbling champagne flutes. Sara Sullivan hardly noticed the group of giddy bridesmaids that had gathered in a corner near the stage.

It was only about the millionth time in her fifteen-year-old life that she'd attended a party where she was neither guest nor hostess. Her exact title was "assistant to the event planner"—the event planner being her mother. At this particular party, it had been hard to focus on assisting with anything. She'd practically abandoned her responsibilities as she became fully enraptured with the cutest guy she'd ever seen in her life.

From the back of the reception hall she gazed at dark curls, sun-kissed skin, a perfectly chiseled jaw, and sculpted broad shoulders. He had the rare combination of dark hair and blue eyes, and she swore his eyelashes cast a shadow over his cheeks. He was new in the band, and he stood out like a palm tree in Alaska. Much younger than the rest of his bandmates, he looked like he didn't belong in the band-issued suit he wore. The only thing that seemed to fit him was the guitar he held.

A crackle came from her headset. She waited to hear her mother's voice, but there was nothing.

"Mom?"

No reply.

Odd, she thought. She wondered if Cute Guitar Guy liked girls who wore headsets. She felt so dorky sometimes.

When she glanced back at the stage, he was watching her. She didn't give her eyes a chance to introduce themselves to his, and quickly looked at the clipboard she held.

Why was she so shy and weird when it came to cute boys? Now she looked antisocial, with a headset. A confident smile with lingering eye contact would've been nice. No, instead she had to be the nervous-looking chick with wire pinching the sides of her caramel-colored bangs.

"I can't find your mother anywhere." The agitated voice took Sara by surprise. Sara turned to face the mother of the bride. One look at her and Sara knew the woman had come with trouble. A vein spidered down her temple, slithering beneath the high collar of her taupe sequined gown, and her pointy eyebrows were all scrunched up.

"I am not watching a ten-thousand-dollar cake end up all over the soles of that man's Air Jordans." She threw a thumb over her shoulder. "I don't care who he is."

A crowd had gathered near the cake. In spite of Sara's five-two frame, she could still make out the tip of the bride's veil somewhere inside the fray. She had no idea what was going on, but she headed toward the crowd, the mother of the bride marching closely behind her.

"Mom, you there?" Sara spoke into the microphone on her headset. "Potential RM.

I repeat, potential RM." They had all kinds of codes, and *RM* was code for "disaster." It actually stood for *Regina Manfrankler*. Sara and her mother had made up the code last year after the ambitious Regina Manfrankler had shown up at the wedding of her ex-boyfriend, equipped with three cans of red spray paint she'd earmarked for the entire wedding party.

Sara and Leah found her tagging the white bridal limo with THE GROOM HAS A SMALL— They stopped her before she divulged the details, then covered her words with streamers and whipped cream. Sara had been pretty certain that what Regina had planned to say didn't involve the groom's bank account.

Sara made her way to the group, and as far as she could tell, everyone looked happy. A smile covered the bride's face as she shimmied to the music. The bridesmaids' yellow dresses swished with each step. So what could the problem be? It wasn't until Sara was up close that she noticed the potential RM. On his back, legs spinning around the floor like the top of a Black Hawk helicopter, was the tallest man Sara had ever seen in her fifteen years on earth. His name was Mickey Piper.

In the world of basketball he was famous. He was also the best man at this wedding.

Sara didn't care if he had ten pairs of sneakers and a video game bearing his name. All she cared about was that he was break-dancing within a millimeter of the wedding cake. This wasn't any old cake. This was a delicacy adorned with rare edible flowers that had been delivered from the south of France. It was a pastry chef's masterpiece that boasted of real diamonds atop the bride and groom figurines. Sara and her mother had spent more time making sure this cake turned out okay than most girls spend picking out homecoming gowns. He must be stopped at once.

But how? This was not her kind of crisis. Her list of responsibilities included bustling the bride's dress and making sure each guest left with a wedding favor. This was clearly a crisis reserved for someone with more experience. She tried her mother again. Still nothing. She watched Mickey Piper for a moment. She knew it was twisted, but she couldn't help but wonder if the videographer was catching all this. How often did famous basketball players break-dance at weddings?

She'd witnessed her fair share of wedding idiots. When your mother is an event planner, brides gone wild and in-laws who hate each other are part of everyday life. But this was celebrity clientele here. She couldn't part the crowd, step inside, and grab one of his ankles. One nudge from his size 22 sneakers could blast her to a chandelier. This could end up in the tabloids if handled wrong. Her heart skipped a beat when the cake wobbled. She thought fast, then whipped around to face the mother of the bride.

"Give me one minute."

Sara felt nervous as she headed for the band, and not just because of Cute Guitar Guy. She had no idea if her little impromptu plan to save the cake was going to work. She'd worked with this cover band at many weddings and knew the lead singer, Kenny, well enough. He was cool for someone in his twenties, and he was really easy to work with. She stopped at the side of the stage and waved her arms. Kenny was too wrapped up in belting out Justin Timberlake to notice her. Then the guitarist's blue eyes landed on hers, and even in the midst of a crisis, she couldn't help but feel a buzz of warm, tingly excitement. Good thing it was a drum solo, because this gave Cute Guitar Guy the opportunity to help her.

"I need Kenny!" She had to shout because the music was so loud she thought he wouldn't hear her. He gave her a very nonchalant thumbs-up, as if he was used to helping out in the middle of songs. He edged in close to Kenny, made eye contact with the lead singer, then subtly nodded toward Sara.

Once she had Kenny's undivided attention, she mouthed, *"Conga line now. Best man must lead."*

Kenny closed in on his microphone. "Who's in the mood for a conga line?" His voice boomed over the crowd. There were a few howls from the dance floor. "Grab the waist of the closest person, and let's shake it up! I wanna see everyone on the dance floor! And I mean everyone! Where are the new Mr. and Mrs. Wilcox?" he sang. "I want the newlyweds in this conga line!"

She watched the bride scream, pull up her skirts, and jump to the front of the line. Her dress moved right along with the bridesmaids' as they began to dance around the room. "And where's the best man? Best man, I want you out there too," Kenny's voice sang through the microphone. "Everyone follow the best man."

Sara didn't have a chance to run for her life before Mickey Piper plucked her from the floor like a daisy and grabbed hold of her waist as he made her the head of the line. Her first thought was that she must look like a petrified leprechaun next to him. The man was seven foot two, which was a solid two feet taller than her minuscule frame.

"The conga line is the bomb!" Mickey shouted so loud she thought her eardrums would burst. When she'd suggested the conga line to Kenny, she never imagined that she'd be caught up in it. She tried to wiggle free, but his hands felt nailed to her waist. All she could do was move. Her biggest fear was that if she stopped, everyone would fall like dominoes behind her, and she'd end up like gum beneath his shoe.

She didn't dance. She knew it was just the conga line, but she'd been watching things like this from the sidelines for years—not participating. Was she supposed to hop? Or did she trot? She took a few hops and felt her headset slip from the right side of her head. It dangled at an awkward angle over her forehead, and for a moment she was blind. She still held her clipboard. With one hand, she grappled with the headset, but the moving train behind her pushed hard, and she only managed to get it away from her face. Somewhere in trying to fix the headset, her bangs had gotten caught in the wire, and her hair stuck up like weeds. She was the Easter Bunny with a lopsided ear.

She caught a glimpse of the caterer's son, Blake. He was usually the only other person her age working at events, and he thrived on flirtatiously teasing her. One glimpse of his delighted smile, and she knew that he had enough material to make fun of her for the rest of the summer. She thought she might die.

Clearly, hopping was not how it was done. She tried kicking each foot from side to side. All she could do was pray the song ended soon. She wished she'd run for her life before this ball-throwing giant with a death grip got ahold of her. As they rounded the corner of the dance floor, her eyes landed on something truly nightmarish. Cute Guitar Guy's gaze was aimed directly at her. A sly smile covered his face, and he nodded when their eyes caught. Hopping around the room like a moronic square dancer with a floppy headset and bangs standing on end would go down as one of the most embarrassing moments of her life.

Well, at least the cake had been saved. She hoped that the next time Mickey Piper chose to do the helicopter, he did it on the dance floor, away from all the expensive stuff. She felt her bangs flopping around and wondered if the situation could get any worse.

The first thing she did when the song ended was straighten her headset and fix her hair. Then she got as far away from Mickey Piper as she possibly could. She couldn't make eye contact with anyone in the room for fear of dying of embarrassment. It was hard to believe that it had only been minutes ago that she'd been praying for Cute Guitar Guy to be around all summer. Now she sort of hoped she never saw him again. It was a good time to check in with her mother. Escape was welcome.

It would take a lot for her mother to ignore an RM alert. Sara imagined all kinds of catastrophes. Maybe that the filet mignon the bride had carefully selected had been confused by the caterer, and lobster covered each plate. Sara could still remember the bride explaining that her parents were deathly allergic to shellfish. The scent alone could trigger something called anaphylactic shock. Maybe Leah was desperately trying to come up with steaks in the last minutes before dinner, and that's why she hadn't answered. There had to be a major explanation.

Leah had been planning parties for most of Sara's life. However, before Sara's parents had divorced, her mother had worked part-time. She handled one wedding or party a month. During her mother's part-time days, word had spread around San Diego that Leah Sullivan was *the* best event planner in town. Some people even postponed their parties months—sometimes years—so they could get on Leah Sullivan's waiting list. It wasn't just that Leah had the magic touch that made everything beautiful. She also had a magnetic personality. She had a way of immediately making people feel not only relaxed around her, but important. She made her clients feel like *everything* was fun—that life was one big celebration. She was, literally, the life of the party.

Shortly after Sara's parents divorced, her mother took on twice as much work. Her mom had been insanely busy, and Sara wanted to earn a little extra cash. Plus, her parents had told her that whatever she saved they would match on her sixteenth birthday to help her buy a car. So Sara had become her mother's assistant. When most clients met with Sara and her mother, their first response to Sara was skepticism. Sara was, after all, not yet even a junior in high school. However, as clients became immersed in the party-planning process, their skepticism evolved into respect and a sense of total trust in Sara's capabilities, especially when the parties they planned were for girls, because Sara could relate to them.

She found her mom in the kitchen, head tossed back, laughing hysterically at something the florist, Gene, had said. The caterers were gracefully arranging petit cuts of steak on hundreds of plates. Everything seemed fine.

Sara watched as Gene plucked a rose out of an extra centerpiece and tucked it behind her mother's right ear. It was nice to see that her mother was having so much fun with Gene, but couldn't she at least answer her headset when Sara called? A few minutes ago Sara had been so stressed she thought she'd be gray by her junior prom.

"Um, Mom?"

"Hi, honey." She was still smiling when she noticed Sara. "Isn't this rose beautiful?" The red rose looked sharp against Leah's pale blond hair and milky skin.

"Yeah, great. Why didn't you answer me?"

"Oh, my headset broke, so Gene decided to replace it with this flower." They both thought it was the funniest thing ever. Sara stared at them. That was it? A broken headset and some horsing around with the centerpieces? All the steaks were here and nothing was on fire?

Gene reached back to the centerpiece, plucked another rose from the middle, and placed it behind Sara's ear.

"Gorgeous! And now you two can communicate." His voice was a hair on the feminine side, and Gene always said things with enthusiasm.

Sara failed to see the humor. She pulled the rose from her head. She knew that her mother and Gene were becoming good friends. Just the other day they'd gone for massages together. While cute in an older man type of way, he was so metrosexual. Sara had no idea if Gene was gay or not, and after *Brokeback Mountain,* she knew that one could never tell.

A male florist, Gene lived for watching musicals onstage and baking gourmet cookies. He shared tips on self-tanning products and home decorating. However, Gene talked about his ex-wife as though *she'd* broken *his* heart.

Like Sara's mother, Gene also had a magnetic personality. He was easy to talk to, and he could find a way relate to anyone. Great conversations were one of Sara's favorite things, and every time she had a chance to chat with Gene, she felt like there was never enough time—like they could discuss the most hated villains on reality shows for hours. His opinions about some of the divas on *America's Next Top Model* or *Survivor* were right on, in her opinion. Sara was kind of curious to know if Gene liked men or women—or both. Not that it mattered, but she just couldn't help but feel a little nosy.

She caught a glimpse of Blake in the corner of the kitchen. He pointed to her, then pretended to hop like a rabbit before cracking up. He put so much gel in his hair that his rock-hard hairdo didn't budge when he hopped. She felt her cheeks turning red, and part of her wanted to hit him upside the head. However, she couldn't help but chuckle along with him. He looked pretty funny imitating her. As annoying as Blake could be, she knew that most of the time he was only trying to laugh with her, not at her. She turned back to her mother and Gene.

Sara was glad her mom had a friend. However, if Sara had been goofing off with Blake, she would've heard about it later. What was Gene still doing here, anyway? His duties had been completed long before the reception had begun. Didn't he have some orchids to water?

"Sara, can you remind the band that the father-of-the-bride toast is coming up?" Leah asked. "Gene's going to try to fix my headset. I should help."

Why it would take both of them to fix the headset was a mystery, but who was Sara to argue? "Sure."

Fortunately, the band had stuck with the schedule, and Kenny was already introducing the father of the bride. She quickly glanced around the room. The photographer clicked away. The videographer ducked in front of the head table, capturing the whole speech on his camcorder.

Since everyone was busy, she decided it might be a good opportunity to slip outside for one second and check her text messages. It was totally against the rules, and if her mom found out about it, she'd take away the cell phone. They'd had a few blowouts about text messaging. However, if her mom was goofing off with her new BFF, Gene, then why couldn't she steal one second to text Allie?

Tonight was a monumental evening for her best friend. Allie was on her second date with the captain of the varsity water polo team. During the school year Allie had hit the jackpot when her drawing-and-painting teacher had seated her across from Shane Corson for an entire semester. After sketching each other's portraits and exchanging tips on airbrushing, Shane had finally worked up the nerve to ask Allie out. Allie was really lucky that way. In art, Sara had been seated across from Gil Brunson, the president of the math club. She'd spent a good portion of the semester worrying as she'd shaded his portrait about hiding his pockmarks and making his braces look even.

Even though school had just ended and summer had begun, San Diego still suffered from June gloom, a dark and foggy chill that lasted until the end of the month. Sara shivered against the ocean air as she popped open her phone and clicked into her text inbox. The soft glow of a patio light revealed one new message. The number looked unfamiliar, but she was used to getting unfamiliar numbers on her phone. Her cell also served as a business line, so she was plagued with phone calls and text messages from vendors and clients, 24/7.

sara,
r we still on 4 2moro?
L8R
Dakota

Sara's laughter filled the empty patio. Allie! She was so funny sometimes. Pretending to be Dakota London! She must've used Shane's phone to compose the message. Two weeks ago Allie had sent her a text asking for a get-out-of-rehab party, then signed it from Britney Spears. Now she was pretending to be

Dakota London. Dakota was not only the biggest diva at their school, but one of Sara and Leah's biggest clients of the summer. Sara and Leah were in the midst of planning Dakota's late-summer sweet sixteen bash. The food alone cost more than most luxury cars, and the party came with a price tag comparable to a small beach house.

Rich and beautiful, Dakota had come to their school after being kicked out of the all-girls private school she'd attended for cheating on a test. She had crashed two Escalades without a license and had been arrested for joyriding in her grandfather's Bentley. She was a trendsetter and a serial heartbreaker.

When Sara had learned that they were signing on Dakota London as a client, she'd tried to warn her mom that Dakota London was drama. But her mom had wanted the commission from Dakota's expensive party. Leah had been dying to remodel her kitchen for the past two years, and this was just the financial boost she'd needed to do it. A conflict avoider by nature, Sara had stayed as far from the whole situation as she possibly could without being unhelpful. So why would Dakota be calling her?

As she thought of something funny to write back, she looked at the phone number again. It was a different area code from Shane's or Allie's. Maybe it really was Dakota? But why would she ask Sara if they were still on to meet tomorrow? The only times Sara had met with Dakota to go over her party, Leah had been present. And Sara wasn't aware of a meeting.

She was trying to figure it all out when an unfamiliar male voice startled her. She shoved the phone into the pocket of her blazer. She spun around, the back of her neck tingling.

"Sorry, I didn't mean to scare you," he said quietly. Facing her was Cute Guitar Guy. She'd forgotten that the band was taking a break. From where she stood, she could see his blue eyes.

"Uh—it's okay." Maintain composure. He wore a leather jacket over an ironed white shirt and a tie. Something told her that he wouldn't touch a tie or an iron unless he was getting paid. He looked more like the ripped-jeans-and-Converse-All-Stars type of guy. She understood the feeling of being forced to dress appropriately for an event. Party-planning aside, she'd never wear the knee-length skirt and matching blazer unless she had to. Her outfit was about as cool as suits could get, but it was still a suit. Sara would much rather be in black skinny jeans and a comfy tank top.

"I was just saying that was a really good call."

She noticed dimples.

"Oh, thanks . . . but for what?" she asked.

"The conga line." He threw his guitar strap over his shoulder. "As entertaining as it was, someone had to stop Mickey Piper from taking out the wedding cake."

The nervous laughter that came from her throat didn't even sound like her. It sounded as though it were coming from someone else's body, and she wished she could shut it off. She felt her face grow warm. "I know. I just didn't think I'd be leading it. *He* was supposed to lead."

He shrugged. "It's cool. How many people can say they've done the conga line with Mickey Piper?"

"True." The way he said it made her feel like less of an idiot. He acted as though he'd never even noticed her flapping bangs or terrible moves. She actually felt kind of okay with the whole situation.

She was about to ask him if he was a permanent member in Kenny's cover band or if he was just filling in for the other guitarist when Gene's perky voice exploded into her ear. "Test-ing! Test-ing! Come in, Sara. Are you there?"

"Yes, hello, Gene. I'm here." Did he have to ruin the closest thing to a real conversation she'd ever shared with a hot guy?

The guitarist pointed to his watch, then to the reception hall. "I think I better go back in," he whispered.

She held up a finger. "One sec," she whispered. "Sorry." A gust of wind dusted the patio. She turned around so she could hear through her headset better.

Her mother's voice came in clear. "I guess we're all set, then, honey! Can you make sure the waiters have picked up all the empty glasses on the patio? I don't want my event looking like a mess. Thanks!"

"Of course. Already on it." Could she look any dorkier? She didn't even know the guy's name, and her mother had already come into the picture.

When she turned around, he was gone.

Two

"Sara, listen. Gene's coming over for a splash." The sound of her mother's heels clicked over the asphalt in the parking lot.

"A splash?" Sara knew what it meant. She knew they weren't going swimming. It had always been Gene's way of saying they were having a glass of wine. They were so BFF. It was like how Allie picked up on using words that only Sara used. For example, Sara had gone through a phase when almost everything of importance that came out of her mouth was followed with "at once."

For instance, if she were to leave Allie a voice mail at this very moment, she might say, "I have to hear every detail of your date with Shane. You must text me at once." It hadn't been long after Sara had started saying "at once" that Allie started saying it too.

As they neared the car, Sara turned to her mother. "You sure are using a lot of Gene lingo these days. Soon you'll be dating." Sara burst into laughter as soon as the words had left her mouth.

Her mother was quiet, and Sara wondered if she should keep her jokes to herself. It was late. Obviously, her mother wasn't in the mood for sarcasm, especially when it involved her dating a man who could easily be a switch-hitter. Even though the wedding had been a total success, their feet hurt, and terrible eighties cover songs were stuck in both their heads. Just a minute ago Mom had been packing up candles while humming "YMCA." She'd been throwing the last of the candles into a box when she turned to Sara and said, "I'll have this song stuck in my head until the next party."

Her mom jingled the car keys. "You want to drive us home?"

"Sure." Her driver's test was right around the corner, so any opportunity to get behind the wheel was welcome. Up until spotting Cute Guitar Guy, the only thing she'd really been excited about was getting her license this summer. Her sixteenth birthday was right around the corner, and she couldn't wait.

She was taking the keys from her mother's hand when Blake came up alongside them. He'd changed from his caterer's uniform into jeans and a baby blue polo shirt. The collar of his shirt stood as pointed and stiff as a cornstalk. His hair was so slicked back with mousse even the dim street lights reflected off its hard sheen, and his bleached teeth practically glowed in the dark. "Hey, Sara, you want a ride home? I was gonna stop at Java Joe's."

"It's fine with me," her mother answered. Sometimes Sara wished she had a remote control that could control all parental voices. She would've hit pause before those words had come out.

"Um . . . actually," Sara said, "I'm pretty beat. I think I'm just going to head home. But thanks."

"Right on. Let me know if you need any rides to events this summer."

She nodded. "Okay. I will. Thanks." They often rode together to events. Blake had gotten his license last year, and he'd always been generous about giving her rides in his new Escalade.

As he headed to his car, he looked over his shoulder before hopping a couple of steps. She shook her head but couldn't keep from smiling. "Whatever!" she called.

As they slid into her mother's Acura SUV, her mother turned to her. "Why didn't you want to ride with Blake?"

Sara shrugged. "I wanted to drive home. I need the practice."

Sara started the car and it occurred to her that she never got to see Cute Guitar Guy again. She felt tempted to ask her mom what she knew about him, but then her mother might become Curious Leah and ask Sara a million questions about her nonexistent love life.

Her mother had made her parallel park the car when they'd arrived, and getting out now was a little tricky. She nailed the curb a couple of times, but at least it wasn't the bumper of the BMW behind them.

"So, someone has a birthday coming up," Leah said as soon as they were on the road.

Sara smiled. "Just a little over a month."

"So, I was thinking we could have a big party. Invite some of your girlfriends over, and we'll have nonalcoholic daquiris, and we'll have it catered by Meiki's. I'll hire that one deejay who teaches hiphop, too. And I'm going to make a big board with a picture from every year since you were born—"

"Mom, no. I don't want a party. I mean it. Please don't throw me a party."

Deep down, she thought it would be nice to have a party. But the truth was, she didn't think enough people would come. It wasn't that she was unpopular. She knew tons of people at school. However, during the school year she was always hammered with homework. Factor in working for the event-planning business, and she hardly had time to socialize.

The last day of Sara's sophomore year had ended three days earlier, and she had to admit she'd faced the summer with a small sense of disappointment. She was more than happy to save money for a car and help her mother out with the event-planning business. However, surfing and hanging out with Allie were out of the question. Her summer calendar was booked with events. While everyone at her high school would be sitting around beach bonfires, she'd be working.

While Sara had helped orchestrate some of the biggest sweet-sixteen bashes in San Diego, she hadn't actually been a guest. She'd been working. Even if she did get the occasional e-vite from some well-meaning classmate who was throwing a party, she had to turn it down. She had one best friend, Allie. Instinct, or maybe it was just the fear of humiliation, told Sara that Allie would be the only person to show up at any shindig honoring her birthday.

"I'd rather just go to Meiki's than have it catered. Just you, Dad, and Allie and me." She found it strange to think that she helped plan sweet-sixteen events in which the invitations alone cost more than ten sushi dinners, and yet her own birthday party was hardly a party. The kids whose parents could afford extravaganzas hosted theme parties with only the best caterers, bands, and decorations. Ice sculptures, new luxury cars, and exotic animals involved in grand entrances were starting to become the norm at her school for sweet sixteens. Sara never expected to lead white tigers on jeweled leashes in front of two hundred friends, but she sensed that her mother was hoping for at least a few friends and a cake to celebrate with.

"Really? That's all you want?" Leah sounded kind of disappointed, and Sara squirmed at the thought of letting her down. But wouldn't it be worse if she was standing in front of a pitcher of virgin daquiris with Allie?

Sara nodded. "Yes, really."

"Speaking of sweet sixteens, I almost forgot to tell you. Dakota London wants to have male models hand deliver each and every one of her invitations to her guests. She's set up some interviews with the models tomorrow, so I thought it would be fun for you two to meet and pick out the models together. I gave her your number."

Sara perked up a little. So that's what the text message had been about. She could think of better ways to spend her time than hanging out with Dakota, but handpicking male models? She'd be nuts to pass up the opportunity. She couldn't wait to tell Allie.

"Watch where you're going!" Leah gasped.

A horn blared from behind them. "Sorry!" Sara waved as she merged in front of the driver behind them.

Her mother sighed. "Anyway, I thought it would be really fun if you took on more responsibilities for this party. I've been so busy lately, and I don't have time to help pick out models and that sort of thing. I thought that since you guys are about the same age, this might be something fun for you to do. And I think you're ready to start taking on more responsibilities with clients." Since January, Sara had been helping her mom with setting dates and making phone calls. *Now* her mom wanted her to take on more responsibilities? What luck!

After they got home, Sara went straight to her room and flopped down on her bed. Her overweight cat, Figaro, yawned, then nuzzled up next to her shoulder. Sometimes Sara thought Figaro was the only sane being in her life—even if he had been sleeping on her leather jacket with the gathered sleeves. She'd picked up the jacket last summer when she'd been visiting her cousins in Los Angeles. She'd found the jacket on Melrose, where, rumor had it, all the cool celebrities shopped. Sara liked things that were edgy and rare. It had been a year since she'd purchased the jacket, yet she still hadn't worked up the nerve to wear it anywhere other than in front of the full-length mirror in her bedroom.

She ran her fingers over the sleeve, and her hand came up covered in black and white cat hair. Furry clothes were nothing new. Cat hair and a messy bedroom were a normal part of her life. Shoes buried beneath jeans, books lost beneath covers, and an unmade bed felt like home.

She heard the front door swing open, then the muffled sound of Gene's voice. Sara decided to take a quick, but piping hot, bath—just how she liked it. Baths had to be short because she got bored if she sat in the tub for too long. She'd once set up candles, poured half a bag of lavender salts into the water, plugged in her iPod speakers, and gotten cozy, with Snow Patrol in the background. Within ten minutes, she was bored stiff.

The rushing water drowned out the sound of her mother's and Gene's splashing. When she was finished with her bath, she slipped into her favorite pair of pajamas. Of all her possessions, these pajamas were her dorkiest. If anyone outside her home saw her in this heart-and-teddy-covered pant set, she would die of embarrassment. However, the pj's fit perfectly, and they'd been washed so many times, the fabric was softer than anything she'd ever touched in her life. As nerdy as they were, they were the best loungewear she owned.

She was tired but wired. She didn't think it was possible to simply climb into bed, shut her eyes, and welcome dreamland. She curled up with an afghan her grandmother had made for her and tried Allie again. She was so in the mood for a late-night chat with her best friend. After five rings, Allie's voice mail picked up.

"Hey, Allie. It's Sare. Dying to know how your night went. Hopefully, less crazy than mine. Call me back."

She felt her stomach growl and wondered if her mother and Gene would mind if she busted in on their midnight splashing. She thought there was half a bag of Doritos left, and her hunger pains seemed to go into overdrive just thinking about the salty cheddar taste. The afghan still around her shoulders, she dragged it to the kitchen. The lights were dim when she entered. Apparently they'd failed to push the dimmer switch up another notch. At first, she wondered where Gene and her mother had gone. She'd expected them to be standing around the wooden kitchen island over freshly baked bruschetta or something else that Gene had whipped up.

Then she saw them, arms wrapped around each other, kissing right next to two empty wineglasses. All she could think to keep from panicking was that her mother was a few inches taller than Gene. How weird was that? Then she thought maybe she should turn and run for her life. Her mother and Gene? She was about to run for it when they noticed her.

Caught red-handed, Leah and Gene exchanged glances. It was probably only a matter of seconds, but what seemed like an hour of sheer awkwardness passed. "Hi, honey," her mom said. Then she smiled. "Well, the cat's out of the bag!" She forced a laugh. "Yes, Gene and I . . . we've been . . . well, spending a lot of time together."

She pointed at him. "You?"

"Sara!" To say her mother looked mortified was an understatement. What? Had her mother expected her to run across the kitchen and embrace them both? Her mother may as well have brought home Clay Aiken and said they were getting married.

There were so many things weird about this that she didn't know where to begin. All she could do was say, "Oh. Sorry for barging in." Then she turned on her heels and attempted to bustle out of the room as fast as she could. Instead of making a clean getaway, she tripped over the afghan and fell forehead-first into an antique table her mother had clung to during the divorce. Her jaw snapped as her face hit the table leg. A throbbing sensation immediately took over, but instead of crying out in pain, she tried to pop back up and announce that she was okay. However, she was too tangled in the blanket to stand up, and she ended up on her rear end on the floor.

Gene was there first. His hands gently reached for hers. "You okay, dear? What a nasty spill!"

Her mother was right behind him. "Sara! Oh my God, are you all right? Let Gene give you a hand."

She took Gene's hand and straightened up. The blanket remained in a pile at her feet. "My forehead," she said, running her hand over throbbing pain. "Am I bleeding?"

"No, but it looks painful. It's already a little swollen," her mom said.

"I make a wonderful ice pack!" Gene

announced. "Any frozen peas in this house?" He scurried back to the kitchen.

Leah helped Sara to the couch where her mother confirmed that her forehead was turning purple. She sat in her dorky pajamas while her mother fretted over her face.

Gene's ice pack was the sort of thing that would've popped from the pages of *Martha Stewart Living*. He'd thoughtfully dipped several paper towels in a mixture of tepid water and lavender-scented hand soap. He'd wrapped the fragrant towels around a bag of frozen peas as precisely as if it were a gift he were offering.

He gently held the ice pack to her forehead. "This way, you don't have to have that rough texture of the paper towel rubbing against your face, and I always like to smell something nice when I've been injured," he said.

"Especially lavender," her mother agreed. "It has such soothing capabilities."

As they discussed the benefits of lavender, Sara sat in shock. Her mother and Gene? Gene and her mother? *Leah Sullivan and Gene the florist?* She liked Gene and everything. Guys didn't come any nicer than him, and she was sure he'd treat her mom well, but it was still Gene. Sara just knew he had a pair of tap shoes hidden somewhere. It was too weird. She didn't even want to think about it. She'd been perfectly happy being in the dark. Fine if her mother wanted to date him, but she didn't want to know anything.

She stood up. "I'm going to bed."

They both stared at her and she felt like she should say something else.

"Thanks for the ice pack, Gene. See you tomorrow." She figured that if she acted as casual as possible, she might make a clean getaway. She held the pack to her face as she turned around.

"Are you okay?" Her mother's voice sounded concerned.

"Great!" She practically ran from the room.

Her bedroom felt like a safe haven, and she breathed a sigh of relief as she closed the door behind her. This might go down as the most bizarre day of her life. Conga lining with Mickey Piper, Cute Guitar Guy, plans to pick out male models with Dakota London, and now her mother . . . and Gene. It would've been shocking enough to know that her mother had a boyfriend, but Gene? It was going to be a crazy summer.

Three

It was Sunday and the sun had barely hit the San Diego shores before the phone began ringing off the hook. Her mom's cell phone sounded like a lawn mower as it vibrated on the kitchen countertop. Wasn't peace and quiet the point of putting the phone on vibrate? Cell-phone makers had really screwed up on that one. The office line began to blare and then Sara's cell phone, next to her bed, erupted into song. It was a bad chorus of rings. The only person she was in the mood to chat with was Allie. She glanced at the screen. It was Dakota. For some reason, the sight of her name put a knot in Sara's stomach.

"This is Sara." The greeting wasn't her

choice, but her mother had said that if she was going to have her own cell phone, she had to be willing to take business calls. Answering the phone like a normal person and simply saying "hello" wouldn't suffice.

A sharp, condescending snicker filled her ear. "Well, I'm glad I have the right number." Sara immediately recognized the low voice of Dakota. After spending a semester in the same speech class, she'd recognize Dakota's voice in twenty different languages.

Another snicker before Dakota proceeded to imitate Sara. "*This is Sara!* That's funny. Why do you answer the phone like that?"

Sara didn't understand what was so funny. Maybe Dakota thought it was humorous because she'd never worked.

"It's just because my mom and I sound so much alike that people were getting us confused all the time. It's less complicated this way."

"How cute." After a brief pause Dakota continued. "So, your mom said you'd be available to meet with me today. We can't meet at my house because my little sister is having her entire dance class over. I told all the models to go to Starbucks on La Jolla Boulevard." At least Sara could walk there.

They made plans to meet in two hours. She was snapping her phone shut when there was a knock at her door. Obviously, her mother didn't plan on waiting for an answer as she let herself in. Leah made herself comfortable at the end of Sara's bed. An early riser, Leah was already sweating in her workout gear. A five-mile walk every morning—rain or shine—was part of her routine. Her fingers were wrapped around the cap of a frosty bottle of water.

"What? Is it that bad?" Sara asked when she noticed that her mother's gaze was aimed directly at her forehead.

"Nothing you can't fix with a little foundation. I'll help you. We'll get you all polished up." Leah slid her palm over the ruffle of Sara's comforter. An awkward silence followed. Things still felt strange from the night before, and Sara decided she would just leave the talking to her mother.

She watched as her mother's eyes darted over the AFI poster above her bed. "Those people scare me," Leah finally said. "I still can't understand how you can find them attractive," she said. She pointed to the lead singer. "That one looks like a woman. He wears more eye makeup than I do. I mean, is he *supposed* to look like a transvestite?"

Um, hello? Didn't she notice that she was dating a man who collected quiche recipes? If only she knew how ironic she sounded. Instead Sara said, "I don't think they're cute, Mom. I just like their music."

"So, Gene's invited me to go to Palm Springs next week to meet his parents. You too, actually. The three of us."

"No way."

"I understand. One day at a time here. I just want you to be happy, and I'm so sorry that you found out in such a . . . such a surprising way. We were waiting to tell you . . . Gene just thinks the world of you. And he really wants us all to get along."

"Why didn't you tell me?"

"Look, I'm new at this. I haven't dated anyone in over eighteen years. I was twenty when I married your father. And I didn't know how you were going to take it."

Sara also felt like asking her if she had noticed how feminine he is but decided not to. Her mother must've had some idea because Sara distinctly remembered Leah wondering aloud if Gene was gay. However, now that Sara thought about it, her mother had said, "I wonder if he's gay" in such a way that could've meant, *Wow! I wonder if he's available.*

She'd rather solve equations than think about any parental relations with the opposite sex. As far as she was concerned, a stork had brought her into the world. She'd even been telling herself that her father and his new girlfriend had never set foot in either one's bedroom.

They chatted for a few minutes about Dakota's party. "And listen, I'm sorry that I told you that we had to do this party. I thought about it last night after I went to bed, and it's not fair. If you want me to handle everything, I will. I just thought it would be good experience for you."

Part of her was tempted to accept the offer. Rather than hanging out with Dakota on her day off, she could go to the beach and work on her tan. Come September, she was going to look like she'd spent her summer in Greenland if she didn't go to the beach. She had a way out. However, she'd already gotten involved and she wasn't a quitter. This would be good experience for her. Not to mention that the beach would always be there, but meeting with cute male models came around only once in a lifetime. She threw the covers over the side of her bed. "I may as well go."

Sara's grandfather had always encouraged her to go into figure skating because she was just the right size for all the guys to toss around in the pairs' competitions. Never mind that she was a terrible ice-skater. As she stood next to Dakota's long, willowy frame now, she didn't feel anything like Sasha Cohen. She felt like a hobbit.

She felt squat, and looking at Dakota's long, blond, angel-fine hair made Sara suddenly feel like her layered hairdo was thick and wiry. Sara had spent most of her life trying to describe the bizarre palette of colors that had come from her gene pool. Her unspecified hair color wasn't exactly red, but it wasn't exactly brown, either. In the summer it looked like Sugar Babies. Then in the winter, it looked more like dirty pennies. She'd actually lost sleep over what she was going to tell the DMV when she got her license. Did they have a place to check for caramel or copper? As far as Sara knew, blond, brown, black, and red were the only four options. The same applied for her eyes. Her mother said they were an obscure shade of blue. Her father said they were gray, and her grandmother insisted they were sea green.

She'd always thought her bangs looked edgy and stylish. Her shoulder-length choppy bob was supposed to be cutting edge, but next to Dakota's, her hair must look poofy. She imagined that Dakota rolled out of bed looking ready to star in a shampoo commercial. Sara couldn't exit the house without spending a half hour with her flat iron. For as phony as Dakota was on the inside, everything on the outside seemed real. Dakota had been blessed with naturally tan, zit-free skin, whereas Sara had accepted the fact that she'd live the rest of her life behind a mask of foundation. If she left the house without blush and lipstick, everyone would think she had the flu.

Dakota revealed two perfect little dimples when she looked at Sara. "What? Did you steal someone's boyfriend?" she asked.

"It's a long story," she said.

"I had a black eye once." She thought for a moment. "That dork, Wendy Pich, threw her bag at my face when I kissed her boyfriend at the fall dance. I mean, it would've been worth it if the bag had been a real Prada, but it was some cheesy knockoff that I'm sure she picked up at the border checkpoint in Tijuana. Try explaining to everyone that you got a shiner from a fake Prada. It was the worst day of my life."

At least you didn't have to explain that you'd walked in on your mom kissing her new metrosexual boyfriend. Her stomach turned at the memory.

The coffee shop was packed, and they were three people deep in line. The models were due to arrive in ten minutes. "What are you getting?" Dakota asked.

"I'm not sure." Sara scanned the menu board. "Maybe just an iced mocha."

"An iced mocha? That's so navy-blue polo shirt."

"What?"

"It's so boring. Like a polo shirt. You should do what I do and just tell the people to surprise you. I do it every time, and it's like buying leopard-print stilettos. You won't regret it."

Sara wouldn't know what it was like to buy leopard-print stilettos. However, Dakota's suggestion actually sounded like a fun idea, and Sara was always up for a surprise. "Sure, okay."

"My friend owns a club in the Gaslamp and he lets us come in and do the same thing with the bartender there. The only difference is that you *have* to drink whatever he makes you. It's a little game we play. We did it last weekend and I was so hungover the next day from Buttery Nipples and Cosmos."

Sara knew what these drinks were because she'd seen plenty of people staggering around dance floors after drinking them. However, she'd never actually tried them. She'd never even been close to a hangover. The closest she'd ever come to one was when Blake snuck her a shot of tequila at a wedding they'd both helped out at earlier this year. The overpowering taste had made her gag. It had taken ten minutes just to stop the watering in her eyes. Then she'd had to fill her mouth with breath mints for fear her mother would find out.

The guy at the counter seemed to know Dakota because when he looked at her, he said, "You want a little magic?"

Was he going to pull a rabbit from his espresso machine?

Dakota nodded, then elbowed Sara. "She does too." Sara was fumbling for her wallet when Dakota pushed her hand down. "Don't be ridiculous."

"Oh, thanks. But that's okay. I don't expect you to get my coffee."

"I'm not. They never charge me here."

Sara felt her cheeks grow warm. She should've known Dakota would get the drinks for free. It was amazing how the world was enamored with her. A tiny part of Sara wanted to walk into coffee shops and get free drinks. Who wouldn't? It must be kind of nice feeling like you're special and important everywhere you go.

After they got their coffee, they headed to a table. She thought it would be best to conduct their interviews in an isolated corner of the store. A private, quiet setting seemed best. But Dakota insisted on a round table in the busiest spot of Starbucks. Sara unzipped her backpack and pulled out the gigantic binder she used for taking down information for events. Her mother carried one too, only her binder was twice as big and she toted hers in an expensive leather briefcase. They both tried to take as many notes as possible.

Each client had their own section in the binder, and Sara had labeled Dakota's with her name and the date of the party. Sara's mother had briefed her on most of the details for Dakota's party. First she'd wanted an Egyptian theme, then it had been a fairy-tale princess theme, and now it was Hawaiian, with an island castaway theme. The party was going to be a complete luau, pig roast and all. Dakota's parents had already put down a small fortune toward flying in hula dancers from Maui, including a man who breathed fire. Each guest was supposed to arrive in weathered-looking, torn clothes as if they'd been stranded on a desert island. The party was scheduled to begin at an aquatics center in San Diego, where Dakota would make her grand entrance on the noses of two dolphins. Luxury buses were scheduled to transport her five hundred guests to an outdoor, beachside reception hall where a massive ice sculpture of Dakota, a full sushi bar, and a host of exotic tropical birds would be waiting.

Sara took a sip of the mystery concoction and immediately sensed something with a subtle hint of cinnamon—vanilla cream, too.

Pretty tasty. At least Dakota had good coffee games. Maybe working with her wouldn't be so hard. It seemed easier to hang out with her in a professional situation. They'd probably never be friends at school. Sara wanted to get along with her, considering they'd probably be spending a lot of time together this summer. She asked Dakota how she thought she'd done in speech.

"Since I missed the final, probably horrible." She sighed. "I really don't want to have to take that class over again."

Sara remembered that Dakota hadn't shown up to give her final speech. Her absence had been surprising. She would've figured Dakota for the type of person who jumped at any opportunity to bask in the spotlight of her peers. "Well, you never know. Maybe you passed." She tried to be optimistic.

"I'm sure *you* did," Dakota said. "I wasn't in class much, but every time I saw one of your speeches, it was really good. That one on how to throw the perfect party was really inspiring. I mean, you're so professional. If I was left to plan anything, it would probably fall apart."

Dakota's compliment felt nice. Report

cards came in a few weeks, and Sara had been hoping for an A. Speech class had given her anxiety like she'd never experienced. However, in spite of nervous indigestion and near panic attacks, she'd still mustered enough courage to stand up in front of thirty of her classmates every other week so she could maintain her stellar grade-point average, which she was proud of. Math was always a deal breaker for straight A's, so she knew she was going to have to put extra work into classes she didn't like, such as PE and speech.

Hearing all this from Dakota made her understand why people liked her. Aside from being catty and sort of an airhead, she knew how to work it when she wanted to. She knew how to make people feel good. Plus, she had a spontaneous side that made even coffee seem interesting.

They talked about Dakota's party for a while. She wanted to know how they were going to get tropical birds to the reception site, and Sara explained that there were special companies that actually rented out animals for television, movies, and certain parties. "A year ago we rented two white tigers and an elephant for someone else's sweet sixteen," Sara said. "That was an extremely rare situation though. Usually animals like that aren't allowed at most venues because of the liability. But this party was at someone's private estate."

Discussing all these details piqued Dakota's curiosity about Sara's job, and she suddenly had all kinds of questions. "How much would it cost to have someone like J.Lo at my party?"

Sara cleared her throat and prepared to recite the lines her mother had taught her for these kinds of questions. "Well, I know she recently did a birthday party a couple of years ago for more than a million dollars. It may have even been two million. I can't remember. I can check for you. But I think it's safe to assume that if you're looking at anyone in J.Lo's league, you should probably start at a million. The performers factor in the cost of travel and lodging. They have to fly all their band and crew out here." To some, the conversation would sound surreal, but Sara was now used to being around people who had millions to blow on parties. Sara had worked on maybe a half dozen sweet sixteens, and most of them cost more than a yacht.

Dakota looked pensive. "Hmmm . . ."

She wondered how big of a budget Dakota had for her party but didn't ask. Money was a subject her mom always handled. Sara assumed that money wasn't an issue with this party. Dakota's father was, after all, one of the most successful real estate developers in San Diego.

Sara was a few sips into her coffee when the models arrived. One by one, they pushed through the double doors of Starbucks. Sara didn't know what was more interesting— watching the guys or watching all the heads in Starbucks turn. Terrence, Pete, Jake, and Travis were by far the yummiest things the coffee shop currently offered.

The girls took a few minutes to introduce themselves. Jake was probably Sara's favorite. The most rugged of the group, he was tan and tall and had shaggy hair and a scruffy face. Not to mention he was funny. He had the summer off from studying marine biology at UCSD. Dakota pointed to him first. "You," she said. Sara felt slightly uncomfortable with her tone. "You look very island castaway-ish."

He raised his eyebrows and then turned to Sara. "Is that a good thing?"

Sara nodded and smiled apologetically. "I think so."

"You're hired," Dakota said.

He smiled. "Great." Then he turned back to Sara and whispered, "I guess."

She giggled.

"Now you." Dakota pointed to Pete. He was a model, and part-time football player for San Diego State University. Despite his manly background, he'd been shy. "I'm not so sure about you," Dakota said.

Sara felt herself shrinking in her seat. Dakota turned to her.

"What do you think, Sara?"

"Um . . . I think he's great . . . I think they're all great . . . I say go for it." She felt herself turning red and kinda wished she'd stayed home. She didn't like being put on the spot, and the whole interview process was starting to seem a little silly. All the guys were drop dead, so what more did Dakota need to know?

Dakota studied Pete as if he were a blouse she'd pulled off a rack at Nordstrom. "I don't think I like the way you part your hair."

Now Pete was the one turning red, and Sara felt so sorry for him. Just because he was a hot jock didn't mean that he was made of stone. The guy had feelings. "I think his hair is wonderful." She had to say something. "I think for sure you should hire him. By the way," she lowered her voice as she looked at the guys. "None of this was my idea."

Dakota shook her head. "I don't want him delivering my invitations with hair like that. You look like a nineteen fifties car salesman. See ya." Dakota waved. If this was a reality show, Dakota would be the bitchy chick that everyone knew the producers kept around for ratings.

Sara closed her eyes, and when she opened them, poor Pete was leaving the coffee shop. She felt like following him out the door but was afraid it would cause too much drama. This was her mother's biggest client of the summer. The Londons were paying for Leah's new kitchen.

Terrence was next. Godlike, the guy resembled Lenny Kravitz in his younger days. *Beautiful*. Dakota made him stand up and turn around twice in the middle of the coffee shop. "Nice ass," she said. "Okay. Hired."

Thank God.

By the time she got to Travis, he looked

frightened. Sara couldn't remember what he'd looked like before his "I'm facing the Jigsaw Killer" face. Was he cute then? Blond hair, sea-green eyes, perfect body. What more did Dakota need?

"Take off your shirt," she said.

Travis looked cautious. "In here?"

"No. In Italy," Dakota snapped. "Yes, of course in here."

"Uh . . . okay."

"I'm just the party planner," Sara said, now really embarrassed. "Again, none of this is my idea."

Slowly, Travis stood. Sara felt heads turning in the coffee shop. It was like a striptease as he unbuttoned each and every button on the front of his shirt. Slowly, he pulled the shirt off and tossed it on the table between Dakota and him. It didn't help that some kind of swanky techno music played.

"Can you turn around please?" she asked.

Sara noticed every female jaw within a ten-foot radius drop, and she made a conscious effort to close her own mouth. From the corner of her eye, she witnessed one woman spill coffee all over her thigh. The lady barely winced as she watched Travis.

He was just circling back around to Dakota when a short, balding Starbucks employee with a lip ring tapped him on the shoulder. Even his fingers looked fat next to Travis. "Excuse me," the little man said. "What are you doing?"

"I'm . . . um . . . auditioning?"

"We're interviewing models for a party," Sara chimed in, feeling torn between scalding embarrassment and a burning desire to appear rational.

"Well, this is totally inappropriate." Mr. Stubby Starbucks Manager shook his head. "You have to wear a shirt and shoes in this establishment. You can't just take your clothes off in here. What do you think this is? Thunder from Down Under? I'm going to have to ask you all to leave."

They were getting kicked out of Starbucks? By now everyone in the coffee shop was watching them. Sara had never been kicked out of anything in her life. She didn't waste any time closing her notebook and collecting her backpack. She suddenly envied Pete for making a clean getaway.

Jake and Terrence seemed glad to get out of there, and Dakota thought the whole thing was funny. She laughed the entire way out the door. Sara avoided making eye contact with anyone in the building and bee-lined straight for the sidewalk. She didn't know if she'd ever be able to set foot in another coffee shop again without having post traumatic embarrassment disorder.

Once outside, Travis turned to Dakota. "So does this mean I didn't get the job?" He was sincere.

"Of course not! You're hired." Dakota patted him on the back.

As Sara attempted to collect her wits, she gave the models the details for passing out the invitations, as well as her mother's cell phone number and the business line to their house. Invitations were due to go out the following week. She said good-bye to everyone and made a mental note to avoid public settings with Dakota London for as long as she lived. The girl was psycho.

Sara was still reeling with embarrassment adrenaline when her cell phone rang. *Allie!* Sara had uploaded Incubus for her best friend. They were Allie's favorite band.

"Finally! I've been dying to talk to you! You are not going to believe the night I had, but you first. I'm dying to hear about your date."

"It was perfect! It was so awesome, Sara."

"Really?" Sara gasped.

"Yes."

"Did he kiss you?"

She giggled. "Yes."

Sara couldn't remember the last time she felt truly excited, and it wasn't even her love life.

"What are you doing right now?" Allie asked.

Sara told her all about Dakota and the male models. "I just got kicked out of a coffee shop!"

Allie thought it was funny.

Sara told her how her mother had volunteered her for the meeting and Sara hadn't had much say in the matter. Then her mom thought it would be a bright idea for Sara to take on more responsibilities for Dakota's party. And her mom had given her the chance to back out only because she felt guilty about dating Gene.

"*What?*" The shock in Allie's voice was genuine. "Your mom is dating Gene? The florist with the red Miata?"

"Yes, him."

"The one who promised to buy you a

vanilla-bean candle the next time he was in Bath and Body Works?"

"Yes, that's my mom's new boyfriend."

"I was discussing aromatherapy at length with him last week!" Allie shouted through the phone. "I thought he was gay!"

"Well, now we know he's not."

Allie paused. "Hey listen, it sounds like we have way too much to discuss over the phone. I'm coming to get you."

Four

A sunset at the beach, a picnic basket full of Italian takeout food, and lots of kissing summed up Allie's amazing evening. As Allie shared the story of her fairy-tale date in Joel's Shoe Outlet, Sara savored every detail. Allie had even let her ask all the dumb questions that had been burning in Sara's mind.

"When he kissed you, did you feel nervous that you had bad breath?"

Allie threw back her head and laughed.

"What?" Sara asked. "It's a legitimate concern." No one else thought of these things? Sara could help arrange gourmet buffets and order ice sculptures, but when it came to romance, she felt so inexperienced.

"I guess a little. But I had an Altoid

right after I ate. He had one too. So we both tasted minty."

"Really?" Sara thought about minty.

Allie nodded.

"What else? Tell me more!"

Allie chuckled again.

"How did he kiss? Slow or fast?"

"Slow." The same faraway look that had visited Allie's eyes several times throughout her story came back. "He was perfect."

Sometimes Sara was dying to meet the man of her dreams and make out until they had to come up for oxygen. It wasn't like she didn't have desires. It was just that there were so many opportunities for embarrassment. What if she went in to kiss a guy and hit his head? She wondered if she would ever have the courage to make it to first base—period.

"So how did you guys leave it?" Sara scanned the racks in Joel's.

Allie smiled slyly. "He's already called me twice today, and he's coming to see me at work later."

"He called you twice? This morning?"

Allie nodded. Like Dakota, Allie was long and willowy and naturally beautiful. However, Allie's mother was Spanish. Allie had beautiful, soft olive skin and deep coffee-colored eyes. She hung out in faded Abercrombie jeans and tank tops. Flip-flops were her favorite choice in shoes, and she rarely wore makeup. Her thick, dark hair looked pretty even when it was falling out of a loose ponytail.

"He's so into you," Sara said.

"Check out these." Allie held up a pair of bright orange boots with fur trim and moccasin-style laces going up the front. Both girls erupted in laughter.

"Those are the kind of after-ski boots you need to buy if you're worried about getting lost on the mountain," Sara said. "A plane could spot those from anywhere on the planet."

After Allie had picked up Sara, they'd gone to the mall. Sara was supposed to be shopping for summer heels to wear to work. She needed something open toed, classy, and comfortable. So far she hadn't found what she was looking for. Twenty million pairs of shoes neither one of them intended to buy were scattered around the floor.

"So has he called you his girlfriend?" Sara asked, peeking into another box.

Allie smiled, and Sara actually thought

she saw a blush creep up her friend's cheeks. "Yes."

"You have a boyfriend!" Sara jumped up and down in her bare feet. She was so happy for Allie. "What do your parents say?"

"They like him."

Sara sighed. "I'll be in college before I ever kiss anyone."

"No, you won't. Don't be ridiculous. I have a feeling something good is headed your way."

"You do?" Sara loved hearing this. Whenever Allie had a feeling, it was always right.

"You could have a boyfriend the second you wanted one. A million guys would love to go out with you."

"Like who?"

"Like Slick." Allie always called Blake "Slick" because of his hairdo.

They both giggled. "C'mon," Sara said. "Please."

"You know I'm just kidding!"

To some girls, Blake was probably a real catch. All money and muscles, he was a party boy with unlimited access to his father's Visa card. But Allie and Sara had never taken him seriously.

He was the kind of guy who'd devoted long hours to working out at the gym and ingesting gallons of protein shakes to build his huge biceps and chiseled chest. His teeth were so bleached they were brighter than Orion's Belt. And Sara just knew he spray tanned. He always wore chains with large emblems around his neck, and he rolled up to every event in an Escalade his father had bought him last year when he'd turned sixteen. Besides, he was the son of the caterer her mother always hired.

As Sara perused the aisles, she told Allie about Cute Guitar Guy. "For all I know, he already has a girlfriend though. You know how it is. All the good ones are always taken."

"Shane wasn't." Allie sounded optimistic. "Maybe Cute Guitar Guy is waiting for just the right girl to come along too. Find out his name so we can look for him on MySpace," Allie suggested.

Sara grabbed a box of thonged heels encrusted in fake sapphires and rubies. They were a size 7, much too big for Sara's size 5 feet. "Look at these," she said.

Allie's eyes lit up. The uglier the shoes, the more exciting. Allie slipped her feet into the heels. Her toes hung over the front.

"How much would you pay me to wear these the next time I see Shane?"

Sara laughed. "A lot more than the price tag on those bad boys. Those are Fifty Year Old Lady on a Cruise." They'd made a point to name all the horrible shoes they tried on. "I dare you to wear those out."

Allie pretended to open her front door. "Hi, Shane. Like my new look? I hope I don't scrape my toes on the sidewalk."

"With shoes like that your toes must curl over the edge."

"They're such toe curlers!"

Allie didn't even have long toes, but they were bunched up at the edges of the shoes like they were struggling to hang on. Allie performed a little catwalk to the bad eighties soft hit that currently fizzed through the speakers in Joel's.

They peeled through the aisles, pulling off shoes like they were going through gifts at Christmas, anticipating what hilarious pair they'd find inside each box. "Oh my gosh! Look at these!" Sara pulled a pair of heeled slippers from the shelf. Large balls of feathery black fur covered the front, and satin trimmed the edges of the peep toes. She could see a vintage icon like Marilyn

Monroe sauntering around her house in them at three in the afternoon, with a cigarette in a long holder and a silk robe. She slipped into them and did a little catwalk with an attitude. "These are Vintage Model with a Smoking Habit."

"They are! You totally need a long cigarette holder!" Allie said. "And your bruised forehead leaves so much to the imagination."

Sara had forgotten about her banged-up face. "What if I ran into someone from school right now?"

Sara's cell phone rang.

"This is Sara."

"Allo, this is James Maddox here. I just spoke with Leah, and she said to give you a call. She told me that you had the booking calendar with you, and I'm looking to plan a party." He spoke with a British accent and sounded like he was in his twenties or thirties.

"Okay, well I can help you with that. What kind of event are you planning?"

He explained that he managed a local band called On the Verge. Their first CD, *Hurricane at the Dollhouse*, was about to be released by a small independent record label. The band was the next big thing, and he'd heard that Sara and her mother plan only the best events. He wanted a huge launch party, and all the band members' parents were pitching in for the cost. Most important, the band really wanted Nick Bones, editor in chief of *Rush*—the hottest magazine in San Diego—to show up.

"Do you know who he is?" James asked.

"Yes." She wanted to say, *Of course!* Her mother had actually planned several events that he'd attended. Everyone who knew anything about music had heard of Nick Bones. Aside from his responsibilities at *Rush*, he also hosted two hours of commercial-free music on the coolest alternative radio station every Tuesday night. His show featured everything that was new and worthy of purchasing. He had excellent taste, and Sara liked him because he played songs that wouldn't normally be on the radio.

"Do you think you can get him there?"

Her head was spinning. Sara had heard of the band but had never actually seen them play or listened to their music. A CD release party? Nick Bones? Up-and-coming band On the Verge? She looked at Allie prancing around in a pair of fluorescent green stilettos and suppressed an urge to burst into laughter. Hooker from Hell was the first thing that came to mind. "I can't guarantee anything, but I'll certainly do my best. I'm pretty confident I can get him to come. I think we can make this party a real success." She pulled out her binder and turned to the section reserved for the calendar.

"Okay, so when does the CD come out?"

"July eighth," he said.

"*This* July eighth?"

"Yes, three weeks from now."

They'd actually had a cancellation, so setting the date wasn't the problem. The problem was that three weeks was hardly enough time to plan a rager. "That's not much time," she said.

"Well, that's why I've called you. Because I know I won't be able to pull it off in three weeks, but with your help I think we could make it much better."

She felt like asking him why they hadn't been thinking of a CD-release party sooner. Instead, she set up a time to discuss the party planning further, then said good-bye. A little surge of excitement rippled through her veins after she hung up. They'd never planned an event like this before, and it would be so much fun, not to mention probably packed with people her age and cute boys. The best part of all would be that it was just the type of event she'd been waiting for. It would be a long time before Sara had a career of her own, but her biggest dream was to become not only the best event planner, but also a promoter. It was one thing to throw a party, but it was another to do it with a purpose. She wanted to organize parties that led to the success of something or someone. She wanted to throw parties for companies that were launching products, or bands that were releasing CDs. When she helped her mother plan a party, Leah always started by asking the clients what their vision was for their night. It was so cool to watch how things came together in the end. It was like giving someone a makeover, and Sara loved to be one of the artists. Of course college was in her plans before embarking on her promoting/party-planning career, but this was her first real chance to get some experience.

"Who was that?"

"The manager of On the Verge. He wants me to throw their CD-release party."

"I've heard of them. Shane has actually

seen them play." Her eyes widened. "Wow! You've never done anything like that before, have you?"

Sara shook her head. "And I think this is one event you can actually come to. We can hang out while I'm working. Of course, I'll make sure there is a VIP list, and that you're on it." Allie had never been to any of the elaborate events that Sara's mother planned, and now finally she could see what Sara's job was really like.

"Can I bring Shane?"

"Definitely. I'll put him on the list too." Ever since Allie's dream date with Shane, Allie could hardly speak a sentence without including his name. Shane was on the brain— that was for sure. However, Sara wasn't annoyed or jealous. With her crazy schedule, she hadn't been the most reliable friend.

"So how are you going to do it?" Allie asked.

"Do what?"

"Get Nick Bones to show up."

She shook her head. "I have no idea. He's been to some of our other events. But I don't think a simple invite will bring him to the party. No offense to the band, but it's not like they're the Killers. I mean, they're totally unknown. There has to be some kind of incentive."

"You're so lucky that your mom has such an amazing business. You have the coolest job ever. To think that I arrange things with sprinkles all day." Allie worked in her parents' doughnut shop every other weekend. Every time Sara stopped by the shop, she marveled over the fact that her best friend still managed to look like a rail. If Sara worked there, she would've packed on ten pounds the first week. Allie, however, said she was so sick of doughnuts she never wanted to consume anything with a hole in it again.

"At least you don't have to arrange doughnuts with Dakota London all day."

Allie made a face. "That's very true."

Sara finally found a pair of peep-toe wedges. In spite of all the ugly shoes in Joel's, her selection was very cute.

Sara swung the bag back and forth as they headed to Allie's car.

Allie drove a beat-up minivan, known as the Zebra, that her parents had generously passed down to Allie on her sixteenth birthday. A fading, dim shade of gray, the Zebra had gotten its name as a result of the destruction Allie's two younger brothers had inflicted on the windows during bouts of sheer boredom. On road trips, they'd kept themselves busy by peeling the tint from the windows. Sara had never known it was possible, but apparently certain kinds of material used to tint windows could actually be peeled in small strips from glass. Allie's brothers had spent many strategic hours peeling away at tiny little scraps and shreds. The results had created a sepia-toned zebra pattern on the backseat windows. The boys had also kept busy by pulling the wire from the tubing on the edges of the leather seat cushions. Sharp, thin pieces of metal the size and shape of uncooked spaghetti poked from the left seat cushion. Allie had to warn every-one who sat on that side of the car to be care-ful of the wire. If someone was scratched by the wire, Sara and Allie said they'd been bit-ten by the Zebra. Each time Allie honked the horn, they said it was the call of the wild.

The car was a major piece of crap, but it was still a car and without it they'd never be able to venture out. Sara loved the Zebra.

As they pulled out of the mall parking lot, an idea came to Sara. She knew just how to get Nick Bones to the CD-release party.

Five

A lengthy to-do list in her mother's hand-writing occupied the front page of Sara's binder. Most of the tasks were phone calls. These were easy because Sara and Leah sounded so much alike, which often made people believe that Sara was a lot older than she was. She'd practiced sounding professional and felt like she was taken more seriously over the phone. She'd spent a good portion of her time chatting with the aquatics center where Dakota's party would begin. Because this venue had its own set of strict rules Sara had to double-check that Dakota's attire was appropriate. She wanted to have a custom-made wet suit with special crystals and sequins embroidered all over the sleeves. What Sara had learned wasn't going to make Dakota happy.

In spite of the ten million things that needed to be done, her mother had decided to take off to Palm Springs for four days with Gene. She was surprised that her mother had taken off at such a busy time. Sara had avoided telling herself that it was because her mother was in love. It was perfectly all right for Allie to be in love—to ditch all her friends and responsibilities to hang out with Shane all the time. But her mother? Eww. And how was it that her mother had a love life and she didn't? She'd much rather be hanging out with a boyfriend than calling all Dakota London's vendors for her Island Castaway Party.

She was spending the evenings at her father's place. In the mornings he dropped her off at her mom's so she could organize from their home office. His girlfriend, Tracy, would pick her up on her way from work in the evenings.

She sat in her mother's giant leather swivel chair making phone calls and messing around on her MySpace page when she was bored. Perhaps her biggest responsibility of the afternoon was her meeting with

James and the lead singer of On the Verge. It was daunting not having her mother at the meeting. Aside from the Dakota meeting, she'd never handled a consultation on her own before. She'd sat in on enough initial consultations to know how to handle them, but the idea still seemed scary. Her mom had felt that she could handle this particular one on her own because of the age group, and she knew Sara loved music.

She looked for On the Verge on MySpace and had just pulled up their page when the doorbell rang. Her stomach twisted into ten million knots. She suddenly felt nervous about being all alone. When Sara answered the door, a guy cute enough to pass out Dakota's invitations stood on her porch.

"This is Tristan." A British accent came from somewhere. She'd hardly noticed James standing off to the left.

"And you must be James," she said.

A little over six feet tall, Tristan had bright blue eyes and shaggy blond hair. The outline of chest muscles was apparent beneath his snug-fitting vintage Western T-shirt, and when he entered she couldn't help but notice his cute butt. He was stunning, and she imagined he had girls fanning him and feeding him grapes on a regular basis. James looked midtwenties, had crooked teeth, and wore a bandana over his head.

She watched as Tristan checked himself out in the hall mirror. Okay, yuck. He totally knew how cute he was, which was a turnoff.

Tristan turned his attention to Sara, and his glance traced its way from her new wedges right up to her eyes. Then he smiled. "How's it going?"

"Great. You?" she asked, thinking that he was in breath range. Even though he seemed a little self-absorbed, she wished she'd been chewing gum. She didn't want stale breath in front of someone this cute.

"Much better now that I'm here."

She imagined that he was used to having most girls bat their eyelashes and gush over him, but Sara just wanted to get on with the meeting. While her experience with the male species was minimal, she wasn't a dummy. Thanks to good ol' dad, she had finely tuned instincts. He'd taught her how to tell the losers from the good ones in a few simple steps. *Does he check himself out in the mirror? Does he talk nonstop about himself?*

Does he ask questions about you? Dad had also shared with her that a lot guys under the age of twenty-five were really looking for one thing. He hadn't said this exactly, but what Sara had taken from his conversation was that most boys were about as deep as a gangsta rap song when it came to girls. It was very important to make sure she found a guy who was looking for more than a ho.

They took seats next to the big mahogany desk in the office. Sara offered them each a bottled water. Tristan took his on ice.

"So what do you guys think about a vintage car show, slash CD party?" she asked as she served their waters.

While they took a moment to ponder her idea, she opened a window in the office.

"Here's what I'm thinking," she said as she sat back down across from them. "Every time I've seen Nick Bones, he's been with his prized vintage Cadillac. I'm no expert on cars, but I know he is. He even calls the car "Betty." Last spring, we hosted a big opening for an ice cream shop called Smoothies." They both nodded in recognition. "Anyway, you probably know it's a fifties-diner-type of place. We called the party Cruisin' Smooth and advertised for people to bring their vintage cars. Anyone who brought a car got a free milkshake, and I specifically remember that he showed up with Betty. Of course, I'll call him and personally invite him myself, but I think we can definitely get him there if we make it a vintage car show."

They nodded.

"I think it's brilliant," James said. "I'm actually feeling a bit sheepish because I didn't think of the idea myself."

"Yeah, let's go for it," Tristan agreed. "What do we have to lose?"

She smiled and started to relax. "Great. We can throw raffles for band merchandise. Like coolest convertible gets a free hat. And toughest muscle car takes home a band T-shirt. It's a great opportunity for people to notice the band and draw in a big crowd."

They discussed the logistics of the party—venues, fliers, the number of people who would attend. Fortunately, the band had already taken care of many of these details. They'd already scheduled the show at a club in Mission Beach that hosted all-ages events. The band hoped a hundred people would attend.

"A hundred?" Sara said. "I think we can get more than that there."

She walked them to the door.

"So, what are you up to this evening?" Tristan looked at her as if she were the most important person on earth. "You should come by my studio and listen to us record a few new tracks for the album."

"Sorry, I have a debutante ball that I have to get ready for tonight. I mean, it's not for me, and it's not tonight, but I have to do some organizing." It wasn't the complete truth, but it was the first excuse that came to mind.

He looked smitten. "Okay. I have no idea what that is, but it sounds important."

Sara took a break from work and spent a couple of hours poring over the *Auto Trader* for used Civics with Tracy. Sara felt really good about her meeting with James and Tristan, but it was kind of nice to focus on something non-work-related for a little while. Looking at the cars made her anxious yet excited. One, she had no idea if her parents were going to let her get a car. Even though she'd saved up, there had been a lot of talk about Sara driving one of her dad's old vans from the fertilizer plant that he owned. The not knowing was about to drive her crazy. Two, what if she didn't pass her test? Three, even though her birthday was a couple of weeks away, it seemed like it would never arrive. As far as she was concerned, it couldn't get here too soon.

"Here's a good one." Tracy pulled a wisp of her dark hair behind her ear before she continued to read. "Thirty thousand miles. Immaculate. CD player. AC." She read on. "It has everything you want and it's silver, too."

"Mark it with a star." Sara looked over the rim of her classifieds.

The good thing about Tracy was that she didn't try to act parental to Sara. She was seven years younger than Sara's dad, and she just usually hung out with Sara.

The front door opened, and Sara heard her father's footsteps heading down the hall in his small beachside house. He tossed his car keys on the coffee table, then squeezed Sara's shoulders. "How do Alaskan king crab legs sound?" he asked.

"Great." Sara closed the *Auto Trader*, then stood up. "But Allie's coming to pick me up in an hour. We're going to hang out tonight."

"Oh." He sounded surprised. She hoped he wasn't annoyed, but the way things were going with her schedule, she knew if she didn't hang out with Allie now, she may not see her again until her birthday dinner next month. Shane was camping at the beach with some of his friends. It was a guys' night or something, so Sara had to snatch up the opportunity to hang out with her best friend while she had the chance. "Is that okay?" Sara asked.

"Sure. You spending the night there?"

"Yeah." She followed her dad to the kitchen.

She watched her father peel open a brown paper package, then remove long, thick orange crab legs. There were so many differences between Mom and Dad that Sara often didn't know where to begin mentally categorizing them. One, Dad was always making some kind of food that required a pile of napkins and a bib to eat. His barbecue was probably his favorite possession, and anything that he prepared on the grill always turned out delicious. On the other hand, Mom didn't even know how to start the barbecue. The last time her mother had attempted to grill something, it had resulted in an explosion. Sara would never forget as she watched two chicken breasts ignite like fireworks in their backyard. Mom had frantically raced for the garden hose while Sara had thrown her Sprite over the flames. Leah was the queen of gourmet takeout. She placed orders at exotic places like Vietnamese restaurants and French cafés. For more reasons than barbequing, their divorce hadn't been a huge shock when it had become final two years ago.

Tracy pulled out some tortilla chips and nacho sauce while Dad began to prepare the crab legs. "So, do you have a boyfriend?" Tracy asked.

The question came up every time Sara was there, which was every other week, so it was kind of a lot.

"She doesn't need a boyfriend," her father said before Sara had a chance to tell them nothing had changed since the last time she saw them. "She doesn't need to date until she's forty."

Sara raised her eyebrows. "Forty?"

"Yes, forty. And then I get to pick him."

"Oh quit," Tracy said. "Sara's a smart girl. She'll choose wisely. And you better get used to it, because I'm sure she'll have a boyfriend any day now." Tracy stirred the nacho cheese.

Sara wanted to believe her. However, at the rate Sara was going, she thought her father would be very pleased. Forty didn't sound so unrealistic.

Several hours later she was sitting cross-legged atop Allie's bed, making a necklace. They'd spent an hour calling some of the ads that Tracy and Sara had marked with stars, even though her father had told her to wait until after she passed her test to look for a car. But she couldn't help it.

Allie sat across from Sara, a giant box of beads and jewelry tools separating them. Two empty cartons of Ben and Jerry's sat on Allie's dresser, and the iPod speakers oozed Incubus. Sara had kept her cell phone nearby, expecting a check-in phone call from her mother. But it appeared as though her mother was having too much fun in Palm Springs to call. Allie and Sara were now referring to this new phase of life as "PG," Post Gene. PG life for Sara involved a lot of figuring things out on her own and wondering if her mother was ever going to come back to her senses. They jokingly said they hoped Leah's new love life was literally PG, because anything R was just too gross to imagine.

Allie had taken up beading several months ago, to kill time at the doughnut shop when it was slow. She'd learned to make bracelets and necklaces on this stretchy material and was always insisting that Sara dip into her stash of beads and string something too.

It was a nice way to kill the time, but Sara had never been a big jewelry wearer, and she often felt like the simple things she made were boring compared to Allie's bold creations. Allie would put stones together that Sara would never consider pairing up. She was currently working on a bracelet with bright turquoise rocks and orange and black marblelike beads. Sara strung one blue cat's eye after a white cat's eye. Simple repetition was about as far as her beading skills went.

"Look at yours," Sara said. "It's so cool. I would never think to put those colors together. I love it."

"Yours is cute too."

"It's all right."

"I think we should make these pieces symbolic of something," Allie suggested.

Sara thought it was a good idea. "Like what?"

"These can be our summer of love jewelry," Allie suggested.

Sara laughed. "Yeah, summer of love for you! Mine can be summer of loneliness."

"No, really, I think we should put one odd bead here on this side. Like one that doesn't match." She pointed to the end of Sara's string. "Like, we'll put a red bead there or something. Then when you find romance, we can put another red bead on the other end. So when you clasp them together, the two beads will join. It will be a symbol of love. No one will ever see it because the beads will be clasped behind your hair. Only you and I will know it's there."

"And then you'll put two red beads on your bracelet for Shane?"

Allie nodded.

"Okay, cool. Sure, I'll do it. But how much do you want to bet that mine will still have one bead at the end of the summer?"

"Think positive."

When Sara had finished stringing her necklace, she put one red cat's-eye bead at the end. Allie showed her how to clamp the clasp on, using a tool that looked like mini pliers. "Don't press too hard," Allie said. "You'll break the stretch wire."

Sara slipped on her necklace and admired her work in Allie's vanity mirror. Even if her necklace wasn't all that exciting, it was still an accomplishment. She hoped Allie was right. She was dying to see what it would look like with two red beads.

Six

"The best they can do is let you wear a wet suit with short sleeves and short legs. I asked if you could decorate it with sequins and Swarovski crystals and they said no. They have to be very careful about what they introduce to the dolphins' habitat." Sara repeated the words from the woman at the aquatics center. "But on the bright side, they're allowing tiki lights. And since they won't allow the gondola, I was thinking we could use one of those buggies that are led by bicycles."

"This is terrible! What am I supposed to do? I can't wear a *wet suit* for my grand entrance."

Sara was in the Acura with her mother.

On the other side of the car, Leah had been giggling into her own phone as if she were Sara's age ever since they'd pulled out of the driveway. It was, like, the third time she'd spoken to Gene that day. Gross. Ever since she'd returned from Palm Springs, it had been *Gene this* and *Gene that*. Sara wanted to know if Gene was going to pay their bills. The way her mother had been neglecting work, Sara wondered if everything was going to fall apart.

"I'm sorry," Sara said to Dakota. "But maybe it's time to think of another venue. Did you have anything else in mind?"

"No," she snapped. "This is what I want to do. I've envisioned this since I was five. There is nothing else. I want to ride the dolphins in for my grand entrance, and I don't want to wear some rubbery wet suit."

Sara suppressed her urge to groan. She felt a headache coming on, and they hadn't even arrived at the debutante ball. Thirty-five girls just like Dakota would be running around at this event.

"Well, why don't you think about it for the rest of the day? I'll think about it too. And then we'll put our heads together and see what we can come up with." It was hard to sound proactive when she felt like tearing out her hair. Part of her was dying to hand over her responsibilities to her mother, and the other part of her was annoyed with her mother and she wanted to prove that she could do it herself.

Sara knew debutante balls were for a good cause and everything. They were charity events, and most of the money gathered at these galas went to different organizations for children around the world. Still, she couldn't help but feel as though they were a little quirky. She'd heard that debutante balls had originated in England a couple of centuries ago. The tradition had been carried on throughout the Old South during the Civil War days. Honestly, she was surprised debutante balls had withstood the changes of modern society. She'd personally rather attend chemistry camp then be in a debutante ball. They certainly weren't for her.

The purpose of this formal event was for families of high social stature to present their daughters in a way that suggested they were eligible for marriage. In essence, these people were showing off their wealth and backgrounds to make their daughters look more appealing to potential husbands. It sounded silly, living in an age when women could meet men almost anywhere they went—not to mention all the dating websites she'd heard Tracy talking about with her friends. She always had to remind herself that the real purpose of the event was to raise money for a good cause, and this year it was orphans in Sudan.

There were all kinds of odd rules at debutante balls. A biggie was that no other girls besides the debutantes were allowed to attend the ball. Last year, it had taken Leah a week to convince Rose Jane Kendall, the head of the debutante committee, that Sara wouldn't be setting foot on the dance floor or stealing any dances from the stags. That was the other thing. Each girl who was debuting invited a handful of guys to come to the ball with her. She called these fellows stags. The sole purpose of a stag was to ask his designated debutante to dance so she wasn't hanging out in the corner like a wallflower all night.

The other requirement for debutante balls was that the girls had to wear white, poofy wedding gowns with long white gloves. The attire was supposed to be very

Southern-belle themed. The only thing that saved them from looking like brides was that they didn't have to wear a veil or a train.

Furthermore, debutante balls had their own committees who organized the events. Sara and Leah were just hired to make sure things ran smoothly and that things looked pretty. There was no creativity from their end. They spent most of the evening following other people's orders and solving petty problems like ripped hems or a wobbly centerpiece.

Sara had barely set foot in the Hotel del Coronado when the head of the debutante committee, Rose Jane Kendall, raced toward her at full speed, looking like a crazy woman. They'd worked with this woman in the past and she'd always made Sara nervous. For one thing, Sara sensed that Rose Jane didn't like her. It was Rose Jane who'd done everything in her power to see that Sara didn't work at the ball last year. In the end, Leah had told Rose Jane that it was either mother and daughter or nothing.

"Where is your mother?" Rose Jane asked, frantic.

"Getting stuff from the car." Sara was used to people undermining her capabilities.

Sometimes the suit, the heels, and the head-set failed to make her look more mature in people's eyes. Situations like this just made Sara even more determined to prove that she was just as capable as any adult. "What can *I* do for you?" she asked sweetly.

"We have a crisis on our hands. One of our debutantes has lost everything. And I mean everything. Her gown, her shoes, all of it . . ." Rose Jane had a subtle Southern accent. Sara had never heard her raise her voice, but at the moment her calm, sophisticated demeanor sounded a little panicked. "Her car was stolen in front of the hotel about an hour ago. She's up in her suite right this very minute. She's just beside herself."

Sara's mind raced. Debutante balls were always weird. But she'd never imagined a crisis like this. A stolen car and a missing gown was probably the biggest party catastrophe she'd ever faced. She put on her game face and spoke gently. "Do you think it would be possible for me to take her measurements?"

"Oh yes. I'm sure that won't be a problem." Then she furrowed her brows. "But, what are you going to do? I mean, it's too late to have anything made or tailored."

Sara nodded politely. "I have a couple of ideas. Just let me see what I can do."

Rose Jane gave Sara directions to the forlorn debutante's suite. "Her name is Laurel Gleghorn," she called.

As soon as the elevator doors closed behind Sara, she assessed the situation. Sara knew that Rose Jane would pounce on Leah the moment she walked in the door. Sara sort of wished she could be there to see her mother assure the lady that if Sara was handling it, everything would be fine.

Sara was already equipped with a list of debutantes. As she rode the elevator up to Laurel's suite, she looked over the names of the thirty-five girls who would be making their debut. On the list was Katelyn London—Dakota's older sister. Just the sight of the London name made Sara feel like ice water had been injected into her veins. At least Dakota wouldn't be there. Listed next to each girl's name were the names of her parents. Sara couldn't help but say some of the names aloud. They were so formal. They just sounded like names that needed to be read out loud, and maybe even with a fake British accent.

"Presenting Caroline Sylvia Covington,

accompanied by her father, Grayson Maxwell Covington the fifth." If Allie were here she'd be cracking up with her.

Sara kept her fingers crossed as she headed down the hallway of the hotel. If her idea didn't work, she didn't know what she was going to do. It wasn't like wedding gowns grew on trees. Even the bridal boutiques didn't actually have gowns in their possession to sell at the stores. Sara had never even heard of anyone trying on a wedding dress, buying it from the rack, and leaving with it. Brides-to-be, or debutantes-to-be, tried on gowns at the boutique, then ordered the dress in their size. These gowns were made especially for whoever would be wearing them. So it wasn't like Sara could rush off to the nearest bridal shop and replace Laurel's dress.

She tapped on the door.

"Who is it?" a woman's voice called.

"My name is Sara Sullivan. I'm a coordinator who will be working at the ball tonight."

She listened to the muffled sound of voices before a very worried, yet attractive middle-aged woman with suntanned skin and a cascade of shoulder-length, dark, layered hair greeted her. Despite her distress, she was pretty for a mom. She had delicate collarbones and dainty wrists and spoke with a slight Southern lilt. "I'm Laurel's mother," she said. Two police officers stood in the corner of the room talking to a man who appeared to be Laurel's father. Both officers jotted down notes.

"Nice to meet you. I'm Sara Sullivan, one of the coordinators who's working here today. I heard about what happened to Laurel, and I was wondering if I could ask her a couple of questions about her size."

"Sure. She's in here. She's absolutely devastated."

Sara nodded. "I'm sure."

Sara entered a suite that was cleaner and nicer than her own home. Miss Laurel sat on a king-size bed dabbing away tears. She was a younger version of her mother, and she had French-manicured acrylic nails that Sara assumed had been applied specifically for the occasion. Something about the nails, and the devastated expression on her blotchy face, made Sara feel truly sorry for her.

"This is the worst day of my life," she said. "All the working up to this. Dance lessons. All the classes I had to take."

Suddenly Sara felt really sorry for her.

Even though debutantes weren't for Sara, this day meant a lot to Laurel. Being involved in so many parties that Leah planned had made Sara understand how valuable big events were to people's lives. Party planners witnessed major milestones—the happiest moments. Perhaps that was why Sara and Leah liked their job so much. They got to see the best days of people's lives, and with all the terrible things that happened in the world, a little celebration was needed. A party shouldn't be the worst day of anyone's life, and Sara was going to have to figure out a way to make sure that Laurel made it to the ball in a white gown.

She took a closer look at Laurel. She looked a little smaller than Sara had hoped, but there was still a chance Sara's plan would work. "I'm so sorry to hear about your car, and your gown, too." Sara spoke gently. "But I think we can find you another dress. And I think everything is going to be all right. Are you about a six?"

Laurel nodded, with hope in her eyes.

"I just have to make a phone call. I'll be right back."

Sara's heart raced as she stepped into the hallway. Please be home. Please be home. She scrolled through her cellular phone book and wasted no time dialing the number of Treena White. She was the only jilted bride Sara and her mother had ever seen in their combined years of planning weddings. Nearly six months had passed since Treena had been left at the altar, and Sara was pretty sure she wouldn't mind getting rid of the big mountain of white tulle in her closet.

"Hello?"

Relief washed over her when she heard Treena's voice. She crossed her fingers and prayed that she was still in possession of the dress.

Seven

Forty-five minutes later, Sara was sitting in the passenger seat of Gene's Miata, buried beneath a billowing balloon of white satin, his *Chicago* soundtrack blasting from the speakers. The dress had a mind of its own, and it didn't help that the top on Gene's convertible was broken. His trunk was full of floral supplies, and they'd had no choice but to put the gown in the front seat of the two-seater car with them. When Sara's mother had told her that Gene would drive her to Treena's house, she'd assumed that she meant in the van that he used to deliver all his flowers. She didn't think they'd be going eighty on the freeway inside a car meant for action figures. As soon as Gene had broken forty-five, the gown had flapped around like a broken sail on a boat at high seas.

Sara had done everything she could to keep it under control, but the wind blasted the dress every which way. She wondered what she must look like to other people on the freeway. For all they knew it was a mannequin buried beneath the gown. She also wondered if Gene was talking to her. Despite being buried beneath the gown, all she could hear was the deafening roar of wind and the muffled sound of show tunes. He could be belting out the entire soundtrack of *Chicago* and she'd have no idea. Each time they hit a stoplight, she tried to dig through the satin and tulle and remove the wedding gown mask that covered her entire torso. But just as she started to make any kind of progress toward breaking light, Gene revved the engine and they were back with the flow of traffic.

As Sara sat lost in Wedding Gown Land, she thought about how this situation had actually worked out well. Treena's kindness had exceeded her bitter feelings about her ex-fiancé and cancelled wedding, and she'd been happy to lend her gown.

"If I can help in any way," she'd said. "I'm just glad to see the gown is going to good use and it wasn't a total waste." She'd held it out. "It's all yours."

She'd even thrown in her unscuffed white satin pumps. Gene had rubbed his hands over the satin. "These are gorgeous! Wow, you really have some great taste, my friend," he'd said.

When Sara had arrived at Treena's, she was getting ready for a date with her new boyfriend. According to Treena, he was a really nice guy and nothing like the jerk who'd left her at the altar. Today, it seemed there were happy endings for everyone.

Sara figured that they must've arrived at the hotel when the car came to a screeching halt and the ignition died. "You all right under there, chief?" Gene asked. He'd been calling her chief ever since he ditched his floral arranging to take her to Treena's. He'd said it was symbolic of the fact that she'd been running things so smoothly for her mother. She wasn't sure what to think of the nickname. Part of her was glad things were going so well with the business. However, she wouldn't have to play *chief* if Gene had never come into the picture to begin with.

The first thing she noticed when Gene lifted up the gown was that his arms were kinda hairy. She'd never noticed his hairy arms before, and it didn't seem like they really fit him. He didn't seem like a hairy-armed person. Any kind of body hair on Gene was something she wanted to avoid thinking about, so she quickly began to help him peel off the dress. As she undid several layers of tulle, her heart skipped a beat. Standing within a few feet of the car was Cute Guitar Guy. She swallowed.

Why did she have to see him during the most embarrassing moments of her life? The first thing she noticed was his dimples. Then she prayed he wasn't smiling because she looked worthy of comedy. Maybe there was a remote chance he liked girls tangled in wedding gowns, with bruised foreheads and no idea how to dance the conga. His hair was loosely slicked and he wore a tux. Was he a stag for one of the girls? He didn't seem like the type. Then she remembered that the Kenny Street Band wore tuxes for certain events. But she didn't think they were performing at this event. He waved, and she knew he was definitely grinning at her.

"Hi there," she said. She didn't have a free arm to wave. She prayed her makeup hadn't rubbed off on the wedding gown. Even though the bruise was turning yellow, it was still obvious without makeup.

"You working here tonight?" He headed toward her side of the car. Softly he reached down and helped her lift a corner of the skirt from her shoulder. Gene took the other end and together they freed her.

"I am," she said as he opened her car door. "What about you? You're working at the ball too?" The debutante committee had hired the band. Sara didn't think it was his group.

He shook his head. "We're playing for another wedding. In a different ballroom. Look at my shoes. I can see my reflection in them."

She laughed as she looked at his shiny dress shoes. She could almost see her reflection in the toes. "Welcome to my world," she said. "I have to dress up in things I hate every weekend. Take this suit for instance."

Gene left to park the car, and Sara and Cute Guitar Guy walked inside the hotel together. He carried the dress for her, holding it above his shoulders so it didn't drag on the ground. She couldn't help but think how strange this all was. Cute Guitar Guy dressed in a tux, carrying the wedding gown of a jilted bride with Sara by his side. What must they look like to strangers? Her cell phone came blaring to life.

"Not now," she breathed as they hustled through the lobby.

She tried not to act too disappointed when she glanced at him. "Sorry, I better take this." She opened her phone, then pressed it against her ear. "This is Sara."

"Sara, ohmigod. I have the best idea. It must be done. Please, please, please say you can make it happen. You just have to make it happen. I've never heard of anyone doing this, and I want it at my party. Can you do it?" Dakota sounded frantic.

"Well, first I have to know what the idea is." Sara said it as sweetly as possible.

"I was thinking, since I'm going to be a goddess for a day, I'm going to need a crown. And I don't want just some cheap bridal-store tiara. Mine has to be custom. I'm having it made by Mikahi Sutso, jeweler to the stars. He's the one who everyone says they borrowed stuff from when they're walking down the red carpet to the Oscars. And I want . . . are you ready for this?"

"Okay."

"I want the diamonds of celebrities in my tiara. Ones who have just gone through breakups, since I've just gone through a horrible breakup myself. Someday I'll tell you all about that drama."

"Um-hmmm." Sara remained neutral even though she wondered where in the world Dakota had cooked up this idea.

She could see the wedding gown swishing from the corner of her eye, and she wondered if Cute Guitar Guy was listening to her end of the conversation. "Anyway, are you ready to hear the rest?"

"I am."

"I want the diamonds from Jennifer Aniston's engagement ring in my tiara. I want Nicole Kidman's diamonds that she shared with Tom in my tiara. And there's plenty more. My little sister's making a list right now of other dumped celebrities."

She may as well have asked for King Tut's tomb to be displayed at the head table. Sara really wished she was capable of obtaining the jewels of celebrities. But she was willing to bet there wasn't an event planner in the universe who had this capability.

"Hello? Sara are you there? Did you hear what I just said?"

"Yes." Don't be a party pooper. "I'll do my best. Listen, I really want to hear all about your tiara, but I'm right in the middle of something. Can I call you back?"

They'd reached the elevator by the time she hung up with Dakota. "Sorry about that," she said.

"No problem. Sounds like you're really busy," he said.

She slipped her phone into her jacket pocket. "Always."

With his free hand, he pointed to the elevator buttons. "Going up?"

She nodded as she took the dress from his other hand.

He glanced at his watch. "I have to run. But let's catch up later for sure."

"Sounds good."

"Yeah, I have to talk to you about some stuff!" he called as he hurried off.

What did he need to talk about? She indulged in fantasies that he wanted to take her out for her birthday, or that he was writing a song dedicated to her. Chances were it was something really boring, but it didn't hurt to dream.

She still needed to make sure the dress fit Laurel. Just because she had a gown didn't mean it was going to fit. If it was too big, they could always pin it in such a way that no one would ever be able to tell. But if the dress was too small, that would be another story. She also needed to have her mother meet her in Laurel's room with their steamer. They took the machine with them to all weddings, debutante balls, quinceañeras, and sweet sixteens. They'd have the gown looking as good as new in no time.

As she waited for the elevator, Rose Jane Kendall came rushing toward her. Sara worried the woman might freak out right there on the hotel carpet. When she saw the dress in Sara's hands, her eyes nearly popped from her face. "Oh, my word," she said in her Southern drawl. "This gown is perfect for Laurel! I can't believe you did it! I really thought we had the worst debutante tragedy I would ever see on my hands." Her wide eyes wandered over the gown. "How'd you do it?"

"Does it really matter?" Sara smiled playfully.

Rose Jane hooted. "I guess not." She reached inside a large Louis Vuitton bag and pulled out a pair of elbow-length white gloves. "I always carry an extra pair." She gave them to Sara.

"I'll take these up there," Sara said.

Rose Jane touched Sara's elbow just before Sara turned to leave. "Miss Sara?"

"Yes."

"Thank you. You're the best."

Sara felt like she was supposed to curtsy or something. Instead, she smiled. "Just doing my job."

Sara found Laurel, still in her robe. The police had left and both her parents were missing in action. In the time that Sara had been gone, Laurel's hair had been pulled into a sweeping French twist. A fresh coat of makeup had been applied, and she already looked better. Her red-rimmed eyes lit up when she saw her. "Where'd you get it?" she asked.

"An old friend of mine." Sara hung the dress on the back of a door for Laurel to admire.

Eyes wide, she raced over to the gown and ran her fingers over the satin. The gown had a delicate lace bodice with tiny little cap sleeves that dropped elegantly over the shoulders. Aside from the wrinkles, it looked brand new.

"Try it on," Sara said. "I have a steamer on the way. But let's make sure it fits before we steam out the wrinkles."

"You are unbelievable." Laurel danced around the gown as Sara took it from the hanger. "I can't believe you found this."

Sara helped her climb into the dress. Then she pulled a button hook from her backpack and carefully began to loop each tiny button up Laurel's back. There must've been a hundred fine little satin-covered buttons. Laurel gasped as soon as they were finished. "Oh my God! It's perfect. When you told me you were going to get a dress, I didn't know what to imagine. But this is gorgeous!" She threw her arms around Sara. "You're like a superhero. You've saved the day!"

Sara was going through a checklist from her mother when she spotted Dakota London's parents heading down the receiving line. She hadn't forgotten that Dakota's older sister, Katelyn, was making her debut tonight. Sara noticed that Dakota had her father's wide blue eyes and angular chin. Her mother was petite and had perfectly coiffed, poofy blond hair. She had arms that looked as though they spent a lot of time backhanding tennis balls. The massive topaz that sparkled above her sage-colored evening gown looked capable of breaking a windshield.

As Sara watched the Londons fake-smile their way through the receiving line, she made a mental note to herself that she would never have a receiving line at any party she ever threw for herself. The whole process appeared draining. Every single person had to shake one hand after another, mostly those of people they didn't know.

They said things like "How do you do?" which just sounded so silly and awkward. Sara had even tried to say it once, and it had felt funny coming from her mouth. What was wrong with "How are you?" Or even "Hey, what's up? I heard you got a new Bentley."

The atmosphere in the room was regal. Massive crystal chandeliers cast a warm, flattering glow over Gene's beautiful floral arrangements. Long, firm white lilies popped from bushels of white roses. The lights from the chandeliers cast sparkles off all the jeweled necks in the receiving line. Strapless gowns and tuxes were rampant. Sara watched Dakota's mom release the last handshake in the receiving line. The moment she noticed Sara, she motioned for her.

She had thin lips and a slight overbite. "Sara Sullivan?" Her mouth didn't seem to move much when she spoke, and her eyes looked bewildered. Sara noticed the same expression in the receiving line and wondered if she just always looked this way.

"Yes. Hi, Mrs. London. How are you?"

"Lovely, thank you. And how do you do?"

It actually sounded pretty natural when it came from Mrs. London.

"Great, thanks."

"I wanted to talk to you for a moment about Dakota's party. I've been meaning to call you, but I never have a chance to do it when Dakota is around, and what I would like to discuss is very confidential."

"Okay."

"I mean, very confidential." Her eyes were fixed on Sara.

"All right. I promise I won't say anything." Sara wondered how she had suddenly become the party-planning confidante. Was her mother that inaccessible to everyone?

The buzz of conversation from the receiving line was loud, and Sara had to lean in to hear her.

"I know you and Dakota are probably becoming close, well, with all the time you spend on the phone and everything, and I just want you to realize how private what I'm about to say is. You mustn't tell anyone."

Sara's mind raced. Dakota was going to jail? They were shipping her off to boarding school and the party was canceled?

"We'd like to present Dakota with her gift at the party and I'm leaving it up to you to come up with a creative way to make sure the Mercedes convertible that she's had her eye on arrives without her noticing."

"Ohhh." She should've known better. "That won't be a problem, Mrs. London."

"Good. Because Dakota is so sneaky, and we wouldn't want her finding out about this before the event."

"Of course not."

Sara caught a whiff of perfume.

"The only stipulation is that report cards haven't come yet. And her father has told her that she must have a three point five to get a car. So if the grades aren't there, there won't be a car."

A three point five? Well, Dakota wasn't as spoiled as Sara thought. If Sara had to guess, the Mercedes convertible wouldn't be arriving at the party.

When Mrs. London chuckled, her lips didn't move. A weird sight, the woman was as stiff as a corpse. It was the same look the lady who handled tablecloths always wore. Sara's mom said the tablecloth lady had been Botoxed to the point of no return. "We've also told her that we're giving her the maid's minivan. Of course, I would never let her drive something like that, but I really want to shock her. I want her to be blown away when the Mercedes shows up." She squeezed Sara's arm. "I'm sure you'll do a wonderful job." She waved to one of her socialite buddies on the other side of the room. "Oh that's Victoria Madsen. I better go say hi." Sara heard the satin in her gown crinkling as she headed for her friend.

An hour later Sara stood in the back of the ballroom, quietly watching as each girl was introduced like a horse inside a paddock right before it raced. Katelyn London was currently parading around the dance floor. Every few steps, she stopped to curtsy for the crowd. She was a pretty girl, but not as striking as her sister. Just like all the other debutantes, her smile looked frozen. In the party-planning business, fake smiles were abundant. There were so many photo opportunities. Cameras clicked from every corner, so it was important to have a smile plastered to one's face every single second.

She was thinking how happy she was that her parents would never make her be a debutante, when she caught a whiff of alcohol. The odor was followed by an elbow to her ribs. She turned to her right and faced Blake. His hair was so moussed it looked like a pool slide, and she imagined action figures sliding from the top of his head and into the little glasses that he held.

"Hey there. I brought you a little something to loosen up." He held two shots of alcohol. She wasn't sure what it was.

She shook her head. "No thanks."

"Worried you're going to choke again?"

"No. I'm working. And this isn't the kind of event where we can sneak shots."

"Don't be such a prude. Take one."

"Really, I don't want it." She turned her

attention back to the dance floor. The girls continued to fake-smile and curtsy their way around the room.

"The only thing that could make this event any better would be if they were all wearing bikinis." He laughed at his own remark. Sara pretended that she hadn't heard him. "Imagine that. Debuting to society in their bikinis. I'd come to every single one."

She rolled her eyes. "Don't be an idiot."

"C'mon, Sara you should know by now that I'm kidding. Why do you always take me so seriously?"

She didn't answer.

He elbowed her again. "So how's your love life, shorty?"

She shrugged. "Same old story."

"You need to get out and have some fun, girl." He eyed the latest debutante.

"I do. I have lots of fun." She felt a little defensive.

"You? Every time I see you, you're always working. My dad tells me you come to every single event with your mother."

Her whisper came out loud. "It's my job."

He shrugged. "All I'm saying is that you're missing the prime years of your life."

What did he know? As Allie would say, he was just a horny pretty boy.

He glanced at his watch. "Well, I should get back to work. One of these weekends we should go have some fun though."

She shrugged. "Okay." She'd never have time anyway.

As he walked away she still felt a flicker of annoyance about what Blake had said about her missing out. Or maybe it was disappointment. She didn't want Blake to be right.

Eight

Exactly one week later, Sara was perched in the back of the same reception hall. Instead of young women in white curtsying around the ballroom floor, she watched as the Kenny Street Band pounded out the Beastie Boys' "Fight for Your Right" while two hundred people went wild. The event was the Strausses' sixty-fifth wedding anniversary, and the eighty-three-year-old couple had personally requested the song. Sara was pleasantly surprised they could still hear, much less request a song like that!

Most of the Strausses' friends and family members joined them on the dance floor while they shouted out the words to the classic party hit. Those who were dance-floor phobic fell under heavy encouragement from Mr. Strauss to get out there and shake it up. She watched as sweat beads popped from the old man's forehead and he bumped his wife in the tush with his hip. If only they could have a crowd with his kind of energy at every event they'd planned. She even felt a small desire to hit the dance floor.

Under normal circumstances an anniversary would've been a recipe for sheer boredom. However, these were not normal circumstances. The Strausses were the coolest grandparents Sara had ever met in her life. She knew the moment they'd requested open bar and insisted that all drinks for their guests were on them, that these people weren't your everyday average geriatric folks. They were in the mood to party. Throughout all the party planning, Mr. Strauss had insisted that Sara call him Papa.

"Every youth under the age of twenty-five calls me Papa," he'd said in his German accent. And every time he'd seen Sara, he'd greeted her with a kiss on each cheek before announcing that she got more and more beautiful with each meeting.

The second aspect that had brightened

the party was that Cute Guitar Guy was on stage. Though she hadn't had much time to think about running away to Hawaii with him, she hadn't forgotten those piercing blue eyes and that dark hair—and his dimples. Just the sight of them made her heart race. Even with sweaty bangs he looked cute.

Sara tapped her feet to the beat of the music as she looked at the list on her clipboard.

Make sure bar and patio area are clean. Check.

Check the appetizer buffet for wilted and limp-looking food. She penciled in a check mark. Her mother had a real eye for details, and she wanted everything at her events to look fresh and clean.

Ben Strauss's toast following dancing. They still had a few more songs before the toast.

Dinner following toast. Make sure the Strausses are seated right away.

She looked at Cute Guitar Guy, whose name she still didn't even know. The band was wearing black slacks and short-sleeved black shirts with skinny white ties. The outfit looked a little forced on him, but he still looked so cute.

Blake walked past her, a tray balanced on each hand. He winked when he noticed her. She was still a tiny bit annoyed with what Blake had said, and she wasn't sure why. She knew he hadn't meant any harm. In fact, in a strange way he'd probably thought he was helping her.

The crowd went wild for several more songs before the band took a break. Sara watched as the Strausses' grandson headed for the microphone. The Strausses had seven kids in total, and close to twenty grandchildren. This particular boy, Ben, looked a little nervous as Kenny helped him adjust the mouthpiece to his level.

"Ah-hem." He cleared his throat, and it sounded loud and crackly through the mic. "Most of you know me as Ben Strauss." He flashed his braces, then looked down at the note cards he held in his shaky hands. "I am Bubby and Papa, or shall I say, Ruth and Eli Strauss's grandson. We all know that my grandparents have been married for sixty-five years." The crowd erupted in applause. "And I am going to tell you their story. Because this is no simple boy-meets-girl story. This is a love story, and I bet that most of you have never heard it. I guarantee you it's one that you'll never forget. It started when Papa was a couple of years older than me." He glanced up from his cards. Sara could tell by the twinkle in his eye that he was starting to relax.

"Papa was living a normal, everyday life when his family was thrust into the nightmare of Nazi Germany. His three younger brothers and his parents were ripped from their house and sent to live in the restricted ghettos. Eventually they were split up and sent to concentration camps. As Papa watched his mother and three younger brothers sent away, all he could do was lift his hand and wave good-bye. He later learned that they were killed in the gas chambers." Sara heard a few gasps of horror in the room. "Papa and his father were taken to a hard labor camp. Five months after being at the camp, his father fell ill. His name was Oscar Strauss, and he died of pneumonia at the camp. Papa had no one left." Sara watched as the old man wiped tears from his eyes and his wife rested her head on his shoulder.

Sara felt her own eyes welling with tears. She looked around the room. There wasn't a dry eye in the audience. The thought of being split up from her parents and sent to a concentration camp was unbearable. It was unthinkable, what Papa Strauss had been through. To see him so lively and strong now was amazing.

Ben continued. "My grandfather was forced to work in hard labor for three years before the war ended. And when he left he had little more than the tattered, filthy clothes on his back. He was hungry, cold, and sick. He wanted to get to Austria, where he hoped to find some relatives, but he had no money and no transportation. He literally had nothing—not even a friend. After two days of walking he stumbled across a sixteen-year-old girl with freckles and a long braid down her back. The girl, feeling sorry for him, took him home, where she lent him some of her father's clothes and prepared a meal of potato soup and bread. Two years later, my grandfather married this girl. Since then, Papa and Bubby have raised seven children and traveled most of the globe. Their trips have included Africa, Singapore, Russia, and China. They have built a successful nursing college, where they have trained many gifted people to nurture and guide those who are ill. With much of the proceeds from their school, they have been able to provide scholarship funds for aspiring young nurses who couldn't afford to go to school otherwise. My grandfather could've chosen to be sad the rest of his life, but he chose to be happy. Every time he hears someone complain about wrinkles or gray hair, or gaining another year on their age, he always reminds them that they're lucky to be here. He is always celebrating life, and as we sit here today, I ask you to celebrate the sixty-five years that my grandparents have shared with all of us." The crowd stood—their applause descended over the room like a hailstorm. Sara wiped a tear from her cheek.

She was just about to turn around to see if her mother had witnessed this incredible story, when a voice came from her left. She'd been so engrossed in the story that she hadn't even noticed Cute Guitar Guy.

"That story was amazing. These people are . . ." He shook his head. "Pretty remarkable. These are the kind of people who make our world a better place." Then he held out his arm. "Look, I have goose bumps."

Sara held up her arm. "I do too."

They compared their bumpy arms under

the dim light. Hers looked small and pale next to his sinewy, suntanned forearms. Then he wrapped his fingers around her wrist. "You have the tiniest wrists I've ever seen in my life," he said. Gently, he pulled her wrist into his long fingers. "I can wrap my hand around them and my fingers overlap."

She laughed. "Maybe you just have long fingers."

"Maybe." He looked down at his fingers around her wrist, then gently let go of her arm. "Hey, I don't even think we've officially met yet."

"I know. What's your name?"

"Ian. And you're Sara."

"Yeah, how'd you know?"

"I asked Kenny a while ago because I wanted you to plan my band's CD-release party. I'm the guitarist for On the Verge."

She lifted her eyebrows. "So that's how the band heard of my mom and me."

"The parties you guys plan always turn out really great, and I thought the band could use some help." He glanced at the stage and she actually thought she saw his long eyelashes cast a shadow. "Looks like we're heading back on."

"You better go," she said.

"Nice to . . ." He paused.

". . . meet you? Finally," she said.

"Yeah, finally." Then he straightened his band-issued tie before he walked off.

Sara and her mother practically had to peel the Strausses from the dance floor after the last song. The Strauss family would've stayed until the following weekend if they'd been allowed. The caterers had long since cleaned up, and the rest of the staff at the reception hall was eagerly waiting to clock out.

At the end of the night, the Strausses and three quarters of their guests shouted "Encore!"

The band had already given three encores.

Sara's feet were killing her. While cute, the wedges weren't very comfortable. She left her mom alone to wrap up a few loose ends in the reception hall and headed back to the car by herself. Halfway through the parking lot, she decided to ditch the shoes, and carry them the rest of the way to the car. She was slipping them off when Ian approached. "Hey, Sara."

Without the shoes, she suddenly felt

very short. "I had to bail on my shoes," she said as she swung them in her hand.

"I had to bail on my whole outfit." He smiled. He'd changed out of his band-issued clothes and sported a look that suited him much better. He wore dark, destroyed jeans and black Converse All Stars—just as she would've imagined for him. His faded Bloc Party T-shirt was cool too. A guitar case covered in stickers was slung over one shoulder. A worn-looking backpack hung loosely over the other shoulder.

"Great show," she said.

"Thanks. It puts gas in my car." He nodded. "I have played a lot of shows and been to a lot of concerts. Those grandparents partied harder than any crowd I've ever seen at Bad Religion or P.O.D. They were awesome."

Sara laughed. "I know. They've just signed us up for their grandson's Bar Mitzvah. I can't wait for that one. Maybe I'll see you there, too."

"That would be cool."

"Bossy" rang from the outside pocket of her backpack. She'd downloaded Kelis's rap song specifically for Dakota. The lyrics from this female musician seemed very fitting for Sara's nightmare client of the summer.

There was no reason she *couldn't* answer. She just didn't want to. She let it ring. "So what do you have planned for the rest of the evening?" he asked.

Was he just making conversation?

"I'm . . . well . . ." She was about to tell him she had nothing planned, when her cell phone rang again. Dakota, round two.

"Looks like someone really needs to talk to you."

"Give me a minute." She flipped open her phone. "This is Sara."

"So what's the status on my tiara?"

Sara cleared her throat. "Well, I've talked to Mikahi Sutso in Los Angeles, and they said it's not going to be possible to get the exact jewels that you've asked for, but they'd be happy to replicate them. They can make the jewels look identical to any that you'd like." She didn't mention that she'd had to call twice because the first time she asked, they hung up on her. They'd actually thought it was a prank call.

Dakota's sigh was so loud that Sara thought a gust of wind might come through the earpiece on her phone and blast her to sea. "Are you serious?" she said.

"Um . . . yes." Sara felt sweat soaking

124

her armpits and wasn't sure why she let Dakota made her nervous.

"Fake ones? I'm supposed to wear knock-offs to my sweet sixteen?" She grunted. "Could I be any more cheesy?"

Not any more than you already are, Sara felt like saying. Instead, she said, "The jewels won't be fake. They'll be real diamonds. They just won't be Nicole Kidman's and Jennifer Aniston's. They'll be yours instead. They'll be special just for you."

"Hmmm. Well, I hadn't thought of it like that." She was quiet for a moment while she pondered what Sara had said. "I have to think about it."

She could see Ian shifting his weight beneath the glow of the streetlight. What must he think of this conversation? Diamonds from Jennifer Aniston and Nicole Kidman? It sounded nuts. From the corner of her eye, she noticed another shadow behind him. It was Blake. Deafened by Dakota's rants, she couldn't hear what they were talking about. She didn't even know they knew each other, and she couldn't imagine what they possibly had to say to each other. It would be like Paris Hilton chatting with the president. They were such opposites.

She looked at them just as Ian waved good-bye. "See you at the CD-release party." He mouthed the words to Sara. She waved, then watched him disappear into the darkness of the parking lot.

Nine

Sara arrived at On the Verge's party with Blake before there was even a sign of a party. Since her mother had taken a vacation to La La Land, Blake had offered to help with some of the preparations. Because of her mother's new love life, it seemed that Sara knew more about the event than Leah did. It was the first time her mother had come to her with questions. The whole arrangement made Sara a little uneasy. She liked how things were pre-Gene—when her mother used to have everything under control. However, life was PG now, and she was starting to think she should get used to living a PG life because it didn't seem that Gene was going anywhere.

Her mother and Gene would arrive in an hour. Blake couldn't stay for the whole evening because he had to work at a wedding, and Sara wished it was him she'd be working with all night and not her wacky mom and her new boyfriend.

Sara's days of bumming rides off people were numbered. She was trying not to obsess over getting her license. It was July, and even though her birthday was only a few days away, she felt like it would never get here. The more she thought about turning sixteen, the slower time seemed to pass, so she'd kept busy by working on the CD-release party and Dakota's party. She'd have to get through the Fourth of July celebrations before her birthday came two days later. It seemed everyone couldn't wait to watch the fireworks, and all she wanted to do was fast forward right through them.

Their footsteps sounded loud as they walked through the room. A waiter cleaned glasses behind the bar. The clock in the corner read two. Five more hours till showtime. Though it seemed that they'd arrived ridiculously early, they couldn't afford to waste a second.

Sara made sure the lighting technicians

had arrived and supervised the process of creating a good glow over the stage. She made sure the parking lot was clear for the vintage car show. Blake set up band merchandise sales booths. The list of responsibilities was countless, and one by one each task was completed.

Blake gave her a pat on the back after everything came together. "Nice work, shorty." Then he elbowed her. "Hey, if I don't see you by your birthday, happy birthday, and good luck on your test."

"Thanks." She nodded. "I hope I pass."

"You will. And after you get your license, let's go see a movie. You can pick me up, and I'll buy."

Was he asking her out? She could never tell with Blake. He had to know by now that she just wanted to be friends, but sometimes she felt like he was testing her— like he wanted to see what kind of reaction he could get from her, or how far he could go without getting totally rejected by her.

It didn't help that she offered a vague and casual answer. "Sure, yeah. Whenever things die down with work too."

They hugged before he left. As she watched him go, she couldn't help but notice that he looked pretty good. He'd toned down the hair gel a little, and he had a body that could compete with Matthew McConaughey's. Then she thought of Ian and his goose bumps, and Blake paled in comparison. Ever since the Strausses' party, she felt like her crush on Ian had grown even deeper. She found herself daydreaming about him all day, wondering what he would think of the top she wore, or if he liked the same things she liked on her pizza. She wondered what his future plans were and if he'd go see horror movies with her. She always liked a good escape.

Sara never had time to be nervous before events, but this event was different. Most of the events they planned involved invitations. They had a head count of exactly how many people would show up. Tonight, she had no idea. It could be ten. It could be two hundred. If the turnout was low, she was going to feel responsible and embarrassed. Just thinking about letting the band down made her stomach twist into knots.

She glanced at her watch. Two more minutes until party time. She was afraid to look out the window. What if no one showed up? She debated contacting her mother and asking how things were going outside, but stopped herself.

She waited ten minutes. When she heard the sound of loud engines in the parking lot, she knew some vintage cars had arrived. She peeked out the club window. Before she knew it, the parking lot was filling up with old, classy cars. Gene helped Leah direct traffic in the parking lot. Sara watched as a turquoise Mustang rolled in. A red Thunderbird and a little black Corvette followed. It was cars galore, and they all looked like they belonged in an old Nancy Drew novel. The fliers that the band had passed out and hung on nearly every street corner in San Diego had paid off. The crowd was growing by the minute.

She looked at her checklist.

Band arrival. Seven o'clock. Already late, she thought.

Sound check. Seven-fifteen.

Prizes for best cars. Eight o'clock.

Band plays. Eight thirty.

Band ends. Nine fifteen.

"Sara. The band is here." Her mother's voice crackled through her headset.

Sara headed to the parking lot to greet them. She found a van almost as thrashed as the Zebra several feet from the club entrance. Rusty scratches and streaks ran horizontally over the blue paint. Faded, peeling bumper stickers covered the back windows, and the windshield was cracked.

Tristan emerged from the back. The frazzled expression on his face was troubling. One look at him, and she knew something had gone terribly wrong.

Already? she thought.

James followed him, looking less troubled but unhappy nonetheless. He was talking on his cell phone, and Sara feared the worst. Another guy with a shaved head and a fuzzy soul patch on his chin followed. She waited for Ian and the other members to emerge. However, James slid the back door shut behind the bald guy.

Had the other part of the band gotten into a car accident? Or maybe Tristan just had a horrible case of diarrhea from stage fright? Did one of his ten girlfriends run away with one of the missing band members?

She turned to Tristan first. "What's wrong?" She kept her voice cool.

"I've lost my eyeliner." He stormed into the club.

Puzzled, she looked at James. He was

slipping his cell phone into the pocket of his leather jacket. "I just rang the drummer, and apparently he and our guitarist are stranded on the side of the freeway."

Sara's mind was in a whirlwind as James explained that they'd broken down on the side of the highway with a roadie who wanted to show off his father's '56 Thunderbird. None of the three guys had possession of a roadside assistance card.

"James, what about you? Do you have a Triple A card?"

"No. But I'll go pick them up."

"You better hurry," she said. "They were supposed to start sound check fifteen minutes ago."

James hurried to rescue the others while she followed Tristan into the club with the bald band member. "I'm Jeremy, by the way," he said. "I play bass."

"I thought so," she said as she glanced at the guitar case. "Nice to meet you. I'm Sara." She looked at Tristan. "Is he always like this before a show?"

"Usually he's worse," Jeremy said nonchalantly.

Sara led the two band members backstage. Tristan threw his duffel bag on a table backstage and immediately began to sort through the contents. After Dakota and all her sweet-sixteen requests, Tristan and his missing eyeliner would be a breeze. She could handle this.

She cleared her throat. "No worries, Tristan. I always carry a fully stocked makeup bag to every event, so I'm sure we'll have no problem finding you the right match for your eyes."

It appeared he hadn't heard her. He continued searching. A few seconds passed before he said, "I have to have *this* eyeliner. It's my lucky one."

"Okay," she said slowly. Was it possible that he was worse than Dakota? "Well, let's retrace your steps. Where did you use it last?"

"When we played in Los Angeles, but I know I didn't leave it there. I never leave it sitting out. It has to be somewhere in this bag." He threw a tube of hair pomade on the floor, then a white loafer that looked like it had belonged to Elvis. An empty beer bottle followed and a wallet-size picture of a girl in low-rider jeans and a bikini top floated to the carpet. "I can't go onstage without it! You have to find it!"

You? First of all, she wasn't St. Anthony.

Her grandmother was always telling her to pray to St. Anthony whenever she lost something. Second, he wasn't Madonna, so he needed to cut the demanding act while he still had a chance to be humble.

"Can't you just borrow the eyeliner I have?" she asked. "It's lucky too. Just last week I was applying it and I scratched a winning lotto ticket." It was a total lie. She wasn't even old enough to buy lotto tickets.

"No." He dumped the contents of his duffel bag all over the floor. "It has to be in here somewhere."

She helped him sort through a mountain of junk while silently praying to St. Anthony. She wished she'd brought gloves with her. She never imagined she'd be sorting through a small landfill. She made a mental note to include gloves in her party-planning emergency kit. Every good party planner carried a kit filled with supplies— aspirin, antacids, Band-Aids, stain remover, makeup, hairspray, a needle and thread, safety pins . . . the list went on and on.

Everything in Tristan's duffel bag seemed crusty, and she didn't even want to imagine where it had been. A piece of limp dental floss, a petrified string cheese with teeth marks, and a ripped issue of *Maxim* were just a few things she avoided. After what seemed like an eternity, she asked Tristan to provide a detailed description of his lucky eyeliner. Maybe she could just go buy the same brand and then tell him she'd found it.

"It's about this long." He pinched his thumb and forefinger so close that an opening large enough for a jelly bean to pass through remained.

"Hey, Biva, here's your eyeliner." Ian's voice came from above. She didn't know if she was happier to see Ian or to hear that Tristan's eyeliner had been found. A guitar strap clung to Ian's shoulder, and he held up the most minute stick of eyeliner Sara had ever seen in her life. The pencil wouldn't even fit in a sharpener if he tried. "You left it at the studio." Then he turned to Sara. "Hey, Sara. Sorry you had to deal with this biva. I swear it's just him. The rest of our band's normal."

"Whatever." Tristan rolled his eyes as he snatched the eyeliner.

Ian shrugged, then looked at Sara. "I don't understand why he needs to wear eyeliner anyway. I have to grab my amp from the van, but I thought I better bring this in before all hell broke loose."

"Let me help you," Sara said.

They walked to the parking lot together.

"I'm really sorry you had to deal with that idiot," he said.

Sara laughed. "I think it's funny. And I hate to say this, but I don't see a happy ending on *Behind the Music* if you think your bandmate is an idiot."

"He's my brother. So I'm sort of stuck with him either way."

"Oh." Brothers? "You guys are nothing alike."

"Thanks."

"So why do you call him Biva?"

"Cause he's a boy diva. Which makes him a biva."

Sara laughed. "Makes sense."

He smiled at her. "Hey, thanks for doing all this. If this gig turns out even half as good as the other parties you throw, it will be awesome. And I've heard through the grapevine that you're the best. Some guy from a cover band told me that." He smiled mischievously.

As he said the words, she hoped he was right.

Sara felt sweat trickling down her neck as she hollered into the headset. She was connected with James. "Tell them they have twenty minutes till showtime."

The prizes for all the best cars had been issued, and she could hardly move inside the club. It was wall-to-wall people, and a line had already formed at the merchandise table.

A decent crowd at the CD-release party would've been a success. A sold-out show would've been a mega success. A sold-out show and people standing outside the door to listen was beyond her wildest dreams. And that's exactly how it was. The car show had attracted tons of people, eager to show off their rides.

There was only one thing missing— Nick Bones. She hadn't seen him and hadn't even had a chance to ask James if he'd seen him. She decided to inch her way around the club. Maybe she'd spot him if she could look around a little bit. She recognized many of her classmates from school, but she didn't know them very well.

"There's the chick who plans all those parties," she heard a female voice over her shoulder.

"She's the party girl," someone else said. Sara didn't know their names either.

She spotted Allie from across the room and waved. Allie had been one of the few people who'd managed to snag a barstool. Shane stood next to her, and Sara thought they made a really cute couple. This was the first time she'd ever seen them together. Both on the tall side, they complemented each other. Allie pointed to Sara, then held up her wrist. They were both wearing their summer of love jewelry. Allie gave Sara a thumbs-up.

She was about to head their way to say hello, when she saw Dakota squeezing her way through the crowd. She was heading straight for Sara. Quickly, Sara veered to the left. She didn't have time to talk to Dakota. Furthermore, she was afraid she'd never find Nick Bones if she ended up cornered by Dakota. The party was open to anyone, but Sara had hoped that Dakota wouldn't even hear about it.

"Sara!"

Sara pretended not to hear Dakota. She nailed a few elbows and stepped on several sets of toes as she hurried in the opposite direction.

"Sara, wait up!"

She was just making a clean break when she crashed full speed into a firm chest that smelled strongly of something manly. She looked up to apologize. "So sorry—" Her heart skipped a beat. "Oh, hi, Mr. Bones. I didn't mean to step on your shoe." He was wearing a pair of vintage loafers and a striped shirt with an exaggerated collar. He was cute in a very untypical sort of way. He had a big nose, but it somehow seemed to fit his face.

"No problem. You in charge here?"

"Well, er, uh . . . yes." Leah technically was head honcho, but there was no need to explain all this to Nick Bones.

"I'm looking for someone who can do me a little favor."

"Of course."

"I'd like to review the band's album in a magazine that I have, and I really don't want to have to wait in line for a CD. I have to pick up a friend of mine from the airport after this."

"Not a problem. I will get you one right away. I know the band was planning on sending you one anyway—for your column."

"Great."

She was a couple steps away when Dakota startled her. "Can you get me a free CD too?" she asked.

Sara apologized. "I really don't have the power to be giving away CDs. I'm just giving one to him because he's a critic and a deejay. The band was planning on giving him one anyway." When she'd gone over the details of this party with her mother, Leah had warned her against giving away any band merchandise.

Annoyance flashed in Dakota's eyes. "What if I want them to play at my party?" she said sweetly. "I'll need a CD for my parents to listen to. I can't just expect them to shell out money for a band they've never even heard."

Something told Sara that Dakota was bluffing. All the music for her party was already lined up. Nonrefundable deposits had been made. "I'll see what I can do."

James was standing outside the backstage quarters when she approached. "Nick Bones is here," he said. "I saw him walk in."

"I know!" she couldn't help but squeal. "I talked to him, and he asked for a CD. He said he might want to review it."

"That's great!" He turned toward the

door. "Let me give you a CD for him." She followed him inside.

Backstage was not the fancy dressing room she imagined that Good Charlotte hung out in. It was about the size of her bathroom at home. Crammed with musical equipment and a beat-up couch, the room had grown hot since the last time she'd been inside. The tiny quarters now felt like a sauna. Even though the band members were all preoccupied, they still looked nervous. Tristan was applying his eyeliner in the mirror that hung near a small card table. Ian tuned his guitar on the couch, and the two other members leaned against the table, anxiously sipping bottled water as they worked up the nerve to go onstage.

James handed her the CD.

"Good luck, guys," she called.

By the time she found Nick again, it was almost time for the band to go on.

"Here you go," she said as she handed him the CD.

"Great," he said. "I'll try to check it out." She crossed her fingers that he'd do more than try.

She really wanted to watch the show

with Allie and Shane, but she didn't think she'd be able to make it to them in time. And there was always the Dakota hazard looming. If she got trapped by her worst client, she'd miss the show. She decided it was best to stay where she was.

The show was a success. On the Verge was much more talented than Sara had imagined. Full of charisma, Tristan was a great front man. The crowd fed off his enthusiasm. Squealing girls scrambled for his shirt when he threw it out into the audience. Watching him onstage, one would never guess he'd been on the brink of a rock-star tantrum over eyeliner only minutes earlier.

Ian, less of an extrovert, focused more on his playing than on entertaining the crowd. He delivered some amazing guitar solos.

She tried to steal glances at Nick Bones. A smile covered his face for the duration of the show. He didn't really seem like the type of guy who would bust out the dance moves, but he tapped his feet. He seemed really into the music.

As soon as the show ended, she thanked him for coming.

"If the CD is anything like their live

performance, I look forward to reviewing it," he said.

She wanted to jump up and hug him. The night couldn't have gone any better.

"Tell the band I said cheers and congratulations. I gotta run."

"Of course."

She felt as if she couldn't get backstage fast enough. She was dying to share the news. The band looked as though they'd just participated in the Olympics. Sweat soaked their clothes, and their sideburns and bangs looked damp. Tristan was already receiving a back rub from a girl who Sara recognized from the audience.

"I have the best news," Sara announced.

They all listened while Sara shared what Nick Bones had said. The information was followed with applause. "You guys were great," Sara said.

"Thank you so much," Ian said.

"It was my pleasure. You guys made my job easy."

He leaned in and hugged her. His body was warm and he felt a little damp, but not in a gross way. She wasn't sure who pulled away first, but she hoped he didn't notice how red her cheeks were. As soon as Ian let go, the drummer moved in and hugged her too. One by one, she received hugs from every band member in the room. Ian tossed her a CD.

"Here. Just a little something from us."

"Thanks," she said. "I don't mind buying one though."

"It's the least we can do." He smiled. Looking at his dimples was enough to make her crazy.

Within seconds the knocks began at the door. It was amazing how putting people under a spotlight suddenly made them popular. Sara was willing to bet that most of the people waiting to say hi to them hadn't even been friends with them before tonight. But she was happy for the band. They deserved it.

When James opened the door, a line of people waited. The leader was Dakota. Sara was hoping to avoid her for the rest of the night, but as soon as Dakota noticed her, she acted as though they were long lost sisters. Dakota's two sidekicks, Cassidy and Mariel, stood on either side of her. Dakota threw her arms around Sara. "There you are!" Sara hugged her back, feeling a little used.

She looked at Sara's hands. "Where did you get the CD?"

"From the band. Look, I really have to run. I have a million things I have to do. We'll catch up later, okay?"

"Where's my CD?"

Sara pretended not to hear her as she headed off to make sure that the merchandise people had enough change. The band's parents were selling shirts and CDs, and the table had been swarmed after the show ended. After she broke three twenties at the merch counter, Sara headed off to find Allie and Shane. The parking lot was still buzzing with life. Her mother and Gene were directing traffic, but they paused to congratulate her for a successful event.

Allie greeted Sara with a hug. "Ian is so cute!" she whispered in Sara's ear.

They walked around the remaining cars, sipping sodas. Looking at all the cars made her more anxious for her driver's license. Five more days! Her father had told her that as soon as she passed the test, they could go test-drive used Honda Civics.

All kinds of people from school came up to tell her what a wonderful party it was. Two girls from her drawing-and-painting class joined them for sodas, and she ran into a couple of friends she'd made at surf camp last summer. Unfortunately, her busy schedule had forced her to lose touch with them. She had a blast walking around the car show with the group. She wished she could throw parties like this all the time. It was fun to socialize and be around people her own age.

"Are you going to the after party?" Allie asked. "I hear it's kinda far. But you can ride with Shane and me."

Sara shook her head. "I wish I could. I have to stay and wrap things up here."

The remainder of the evening sent her in all kinds of directions. Little by little the crowd dissipated and soon the parking lot was a ghost town. Her only regret of the evening was that she never got to say goodbye to Ian.

Ten

Her phone rang at the crack of dawn the next morning. "Dakota," she whispered to herself. Couldn't she just have a few minutes to bask in the afterglow of the successful CD-release party?

"This is Sara." Her voice sounded groggy.

"Good morning, new best friend."

Best friend? Was she still asleep and trapped in the midst of a very bizarre dream? When she heard Figaro purring next to her, she knew this was no dream. What did she want?

"So, I have something I need to add to my list of party requests . . ." Bingo! "I need a favor from you. A *big* favor. And this . . . *this* is more important than anything else.

After the disappointment my family and I have suffered over my crown, I think you owe me this one."

"Okay." Sara didn't know whether to laugh out loud or tell her to go find someone else to plan her party.

"I was thinking about it last night at the after party, and I just can't show up to my own party without a date. That's so . . . I don't know . . . pathetic. Showing up dateless is something a party planner would do—not the birthday girl.

"So, are you going to help me with this?"

How could Sara answer this one without starting World War III? "I'm really more focused on planning the party . . ."

"Good. I'm glad you're on board."

"Uh, but I—"

"So I've found the perfect date for myself and *you* have the power to set me up with him."

She had *the power*? It was nice to think that she had power, but she was totally inexperienced in the matchmaking arena.

Dakota continued. "I want the guy from the band."

Tristan was perfect for her. If she'd been asked to create the perfect guy for Dakota, she couldn't have made a better match. If Tristan was all she wanted, it wouldn't be a problem. Dakota seemed like she was totally his type too. This would be easy, and best of all it might give her an excuse to see Ian, too. It was great. "That shouldn't be a problem. As far as I know he doesn't have a girlfriend." Maybe just ten, she thought.

"I just knew the moment I saw him I had to have him." She spoke of him as if he were a Louis Vuitton handbag that she planned to purchase. "I can't remember his name, but he's so different from all the other guys I've dated. After he gave me a CD, he told me that something I said was really *insightful*. I mean, no guy has ever commented about my thoughts before. They usually just love me for my body and my looks. And even though I only talked to him for a grand total of five minutes, I really felt a connection with him. He's so talented. I mean, the way he plays the guitar. What a real talent he has. How many people can claim to do that?"

The words left skid marks across Sara's ears. Whoa! Whoa! Whoa! Slow down. "The guitar?" she asked.

"Uh, yeah. Duh. You didn't think I was

talking about the drummer, did you? I wouldn't touch that raggedy-looking specimen for ten million dollars. I mean, I think the guy probably has a colony of rodents living inside his 'fro. And the lead singer. Well, he's cute, but he kissed Ashley Thompson behind an oak tree last night at the after party. From what I understand, they both woke up with a raging case of poison oak this morning. And I'm really looking for someone deeper anyway. I'm done with jerks. As I approach this new milestone in my life, I've grown wiser and older. It's a new me. I'm starting over, and I want to start over with the guitarist from On the Verge."

She wanted to be set up with Ian? And she wanted Sara to do it? This had to be a bad dream. Sara sat up in bed. What could she say? *No, actually I have a little thing for the guitar player, so I won't do it.* Dakota would never quit laughing. And did Sara really have a shot at Ian anyway? Sure, he was flirtatious, but so was Blake. Maybe Ian was just a friend, like Blake. And tons of girls probably wanted Ian, so why would he like Sara?

"I thought you wanted On the Verge to *play* at your party," Sara said. "How will he be your date if he's in the band?"

"Uh. No kidding. That would never work."

"Then who would you like to play at your party?" Sara thought that changing the subject might just make the entire situation with Ian go away.

"I don't know. It's not important now. Just hire that deejay who teaches hip-hop. What's important right now is setting me up with the guitar player. So, I was thinking that we need to have a little soiree. We can have it at my pool house. My parents are going to be in the Bahamas all weekend. I'll let you organize."

Sara thought for a moment. The last thing she wanted to do was call Ian on Dakota's behalf and organize a little "soiree." "I have his manager's number," she suggested. "Why don't you just call him and ask for Ian's number? That's his name, by the way—Ian. Then you can just invite him yourself."

"Ugh, are you kidding me right now? I can't do that! That is so against the rules. No guy wants to be chased, dummy. The girl is much more desirable when she seems less accessible."

Maybe Dakota was right. Every guy at

school was in love with her, so she must know a thing or too about snagging them.

"Dakota, don't you think it's going to look weird if I call him? That just seems so . . . I don't know . . . second grade."

"Why? He doesn't have to know what we're up to. All you have to do is get him here and I'll do the rest."

"What if he says no? What if he doesn't even want to come?"

"I've already thought of that." She paused before continuing. "Tell him my father has a vintage fifty-seven Gibson Les Paul that needs to be tuned. He can tune it and even play it if he wants. Trust me, he'll be here."

"You have a guitar?"

"No, but Ian doesn't have to know that. Don't say anything, but I'm bidding on eBay right now. I'll have that fifty-seven Les Paul by the weekend."

"Oh." Sara couldn't say anything even if she'd wanted to. She was speechless.

Later that afternoon, Sara headed to the kitchen. She could hear her mother and Gene. She imagined that they were either having a splash or discussing their next getaway to

Palm Springs. It would be the perfect time to tell her mother that she was finished with Dakota's party. The responsibility was all her mother's now. If she quit, then she wouldn't have to deal with Dakota's demands. She wouldn't have to call Ian, and this whole miserable situation would be over with. As far as she was concerned, a line had been crossed. She didn't mind hunting down jewels-to-the-stars, but she wasn't going to call Ian on Dakota's behalf. And it wasn't even because she liked him. It was because this wasn't elementary school, and matchmaking wasn't part of the job. What had happened to the days of answering phones and booking appointments?

She found Gene and her mother hovering over a pile of tile samples.

"I love the mosaics," Gene said. "I'm a freak for those earthy colors. And with the stainless appliances, this place is going to be a page out of *Better Homes and Gardens*."

"I'm not sure." Her mom held a piece of stone. "I'm still debating over granite."

"Granite schmanite." Gene waved a hand. "You place one hot item on it, honey, and it's going to look like the inside of an eighty-year-old Crock-Pot. In five years, all this granite is going to be like shag carpets."

Sara thought their conversations were so boring sometimes. What a horrible way to spend your afternoon, she thought. Discussing countertops? Who cared?

"Oh good, we thought you were still asleep!" her mom said as soon as she noticed her. "We need your opinion on something."

Sara looked at the pile of tile samples, then at her mother. "Do you like this?" Leah pointed to a small object that looked like a piece of polished rock. "Or do you like this?" Then she laid a bunch of tiny little tile pieces held together on a floppy grid.

Sara shrugged. "I guess that one." She pointed to the tiny pieces.

Her mom smiled. "We're leaning more toward that."

Sara noticed a twinkle in her mother's eye as she held the sample up next to their kitchen sink. How could she tell her mom she was backing out of Dakota's party now? She'd already begun the kitchen remodel, and the commission from the London event had been factored into the cost. What if Sara quit and it backfired? What if Dakota got mad and hired someone else? All of mom's kitchen dreams would go right down the garbage disposal.

Gene rubbed Sara's shoulders. "You look stressed." He squeezed her back with his hands. "You know what we all need?"

Sara and Leah waited.

"Facials!" he exclaimed.

Leah nodded. "I so agree!" She turned to Sara. "What's up?"

For a moment she debated spilling everything and announcing her resignation right then and there. "Nothing."

"How's the London event going?"

"Fine," she lied.

"Good. I am so glad you're taking on more responsibility with clients. You're doing such an amazing job. I can't tell you how much it's helped."

Gene nodded. "That was some party last night. You rocked it, chief."

Leah held up the tile sample and observed it under the light. "I made reservations for Meiki's on Thursday," she said.

"Someone has a birthday coming up!" Gene sang the words.

Mom set down the tile sample. "Are you nervous for your test?"

Sara shook her head. The truth was,

she'd hardly thought about it. She had a million other things to worry about. She felt like she should be overjoyed that her sixteenth birthday was right around the corner, but the only thing she felt was anxiety.

"You can take the test in my car if you'd like," Gene said. "It's a lot smaller than the SUV. That Miata can three-point-turn on a diamond."

"That's okay. But thanks." She headed back to her room. She couldn't back out of Dakota's party now. For better or worse, she was stuck.

Eleven

"There is *no way* that guy is going to go for her," Allie said. "Trust me on this one."

They were in the Zebra, heading to Meiki's for Sara's birthday dinner, and Sara was behind the wheel. It had been a monumental day for many reasons. Not only was she officially sixteen, but they'd just left the DMV, where Sara had passed her driver's test! Allie had met Sara and Leah at the DMV with a dozen pink roses for Sara.

The possession of her driver's license was like holding a ticket for a temporary trip to cloud nine. Furthermore, report cards came, and she had mostly A's, with only two B's, in math and PE. She couldn't help it if she forgot to bring clean gym clothes to school a few times. Sports had never really been her strong suit. She'd looked at her report card at least twenty times and felt this only helped her case to get a Civic. How could her parents say no with such good grades?

However, Sara still felt torn between sheer bliss and aching nervousness. Even getting her driver's license couldn't get rid of her Ian-and-Dakota anxiety.

"I don't know." Sara shook her head. "Dakota said they had a *real connection*. And every other guy on the planet likes her, so why wouldn't Ian?" She sighed. "It doesn't matter anyway. If Ian liked me, don't you think he would've done something about it by now? It's obvious that he just wants to be friends. Who am I to stand in the way of Dakota's dating him? For all I know, they could be soul mates."

Allie shook her head. "Dakota is not his soul mate," she said firmly. "I mean, please. Listen to what you're saying. Maybe he's just waiting for the right opportunity to make a move with you. I mean, maybe he just hasn't had a chance."

"I've seen him, like, three times in the past two months. He's had plenty of opportunities."

Allie paused. "It's not like you're the most accessible person."

Sara glanced at her. "What do you mean?"

"Well, okay . . . for example . . . that night he was waiting to talk to you and Dakota called. And then at the CD-release party, Shane said that if he had to describe you, he would say you're a big black blur. Because your black outfit was just one big blur as you raced all over the party. It's not like Ian's going to ask you out when you've got someone else's voice coming in the other ear on your headset every two seconds."

Sara thought for a moment. Allie had a point. She'd been too busy to realize how busy she was. Suddenly, she felt filled with dread. "I've totally ruined it. It's my fault all this has happened. If I had just taken one second to think about something else other than parties, I wouldn't be in this situation. And now he's going to fall in love with Dakota. I just hate to see him go for someone like her."

Allie laughed. "Stop. That's not going to happen, and if he does fall in love with her, which he won't, then I'd think he was missing part of his brain."

"Did I tell you I went on eBay to look up that guitar?"

Allie shook her head.

"Yeah, and there she was. The highest bidder. Her eBay name is Royal London."

"It should be Royal Pain in the Ass."

Sara laughed. "Ha! No kidding. And guess how much the guitar was. You'll never guess."

"Five hundred dollars."

Sara laughed. "Try twenty thousand!"

"What!" Allie yelled. "How much money does that girl have? I can't even wrap my mind around that amount of money! That's a whole semester at a private college! And she bought a guitar just so she can get some guy to come to her house?"

"I'm telling you, she's nuts. But she doesn't act that way in front of guys. It's like she knows she's nuts, and she turns on a sanity switch when she wants to impress someone."

Allie thought for a moment. "Okay, here's what you do. You call Ian and just be straight with him. Just tell him she's wacky and you're working for her, so you have to go along with it. He doesn't have to commit to anything, but you just had to throw it out there, so you can tell Dakota you're doing your job. If he agrees to meet up with her, which he'd have to be just as crazy to do, then you know the guy's nuts too. And they can have each other. But he never will."

"What if it gets back to Dakota that I did that? My mother will kill me. I mean, I'll be dead. You'll be writing my obituary. She's already put down as much as that guitar was for her new kitchen."

"Well, then just go along with it. I mean, all she asked you to do was invite him to some party at her house, so just do it. Keep in mind, he'll never go for her. Let her find that out for herself."

Sara sank into her seat. She wasn't so sure. Almost everyone fell for Dakota.

As they pulled into Meiki's, the tune of "Bossy" came from inside Sara's bag. It was a London. She wasn't sure which one, because the parents had been calling her too. She'd programmed all their numbers to the song.

She waited to park before she picked up the phone. "Hi, Sara. It's Sylvie London."

"Oh, hi, Mrs. London. What can I do for you?"

"I tried to get ahold of your mother, but she seems to be a very busy woman."

Tell me about it, Sara felt like saying.

"Anyway, I'm calling because I wanted to continue our conversation about what we discussed at my daughter's debutante ball. Dakota's getting a pedicure, so I thought I better call you while I have the chance."

"Certainly."

She sighed. "Report cards came yesterday, and her grades were great! Honor roll! She's never made honor roll."

Sara's jaw dropped. "Really?" It took all her power not to sound shocked.

"Yes, we're so proud. She's earned every inch of that Mercedes."

Sara knew Dakota was up to something, but she didn't know what. Somehow, she'd forged a report card. Sara knew for a fact that she'd almost failed speech. There was no way she'd made honor roll.

"So, we've decided to get her the Mercedes SL. You know, the sporty convertible?"

"Okay."

Sara had no idea. She'd been browsing the used car section of the classifieds for a sensible four-door sedan and thinking of ways to fumigate the fertilizer van just in case. So no, she wasn't at all familiar with Mercedes convertibles.

Sylvie London continued. "Anyway, I still don't want her to have any idea that she's getting a car." An evil chuckle came from Sylvie's end. "We're really going to pull one over on her. So I was hoping you could think of the perfect time to present her with the car. I figured you know the party schedule better than anyone."

"Sure, that won't be a problem at all. We'll make it the perfect surprise."

"Great!"

They chatted for a couple more minutes about party details before saying good-bye. She turned to Allie. "She's getting the Mercedes convertible she wanted. I don't know how she did it, but somehow she must've forged her report card."

"You mean they don't want the Zebra?"

"'Fraid not."

"Whatever, she can have her car and her twenty-thousand-dollar guitar, but she'll never have any depth or intelligence. You can't pay for a good personality."

"It's so true. And she'll just end up with people who are just like her in the long run."

"I didn't want to tell you this, but I got the invitation to the party," Allie said. "Hand delivered."

"You're kidding. Do you even know her that well?"

Allie shook her head. "No more than you did before the summer."

"Are you going to go?"

"Hell no!" Allie looked mortified. "Do you really think I would have any interest?"

"I can't believe she even invited you."

"I think she invited the entire school. Everyone from school who comes into the doughnut shop talks about what they're going to wear to her party."

It stung to hear this, and Sara sort of wished the whole school would boycott Dakota's party.

"The invitation came with this little wrist lei that you have to wear to get into the party."

"I know," Sara said glumly.

"Shane used his to tie a trash bag the other night," Allie added as consolation.

"He did?" This lifted Sara's spirits a little. At least she had a couple of comrades. Sara saw her father standing outside the restaurant. "There they are." She pointed. Gene was following him into the restaurant. Next to Gene was Tracy. Sara's mother looked like she was laughing at something

Tracey had said. If she didn't know them, she'd think they were two couples having dinner together. No one would ever know divorce came into the equation.

But for Sara the whole situation felt a little strange. In the past, Sara had often wondered what Allie thought of her family. Sara's divorced workaholic parents and their quirky significant others were nothing like Allie's normal family. Her dad called family meetings. Her parents still held hands, and her mom was always waiting at home for the kids with after-school snacks—unlike Sara's mom, who was usually in her stilettos and ranting into a headset when Sara came home from school.

Allie had to wait for Sara to come let her out of the car. For no apparent reason, the passenger-side door no longer opened from the inside.

"I feel like we're on a date," Sara said as she opened Allie's door. "Does this mean I have to pay for your dinner?"

Allie giggled, then stopped when she noticed Sara's neck. "You're not wearing your necklace."

Sara ran her fingers over the bare spot on her chest. "Oh, yeah. I don't know. It's just a reminder of my nonexistent, totally screwed-up love life."

Allie sighed. "With an attitude like that, how will anything ever change? Haven't you ever heard of positive thinking?"

"I can't think up a boyfriend, Allie." Allie climbed from the car.

Luckily, there wasn't much chance to talk about the necklace. It wasn't like it was a big deal. Sara just felt like every time she glanced at the necklace, it reminded her of the missing bead and how when she'd made the necklace, she'd had Ian in mind. Now, Ian was as good as unavailable. She just didn't feel like wearing it anymore.

Her parents were waiting by the hostess stand when Sara and Allie arrived. "Happy birthday!" Tracy threw her arms around Sara. "And congratulations! One hundred percent! I had to take mine twice in high school."

Gene gave Sara a pat on the back. "We'll never see you again, my dear. So we have to enjoy this dinner."

They ate at a table instead of at the sushi bar. Even though they had a large group and a table was ideal, Sara had been sort of hoping they would eat at the bar. That way, everyone could talk only to the person directly next to them. Conversation would be limited. Eating at the bar would save them from all kinds of awkward moments that could be created as a result of table dining. Gene and her father sitting down at the same table was cause for anxiety. They had about as much in common as kittens and alligators.

Her father ripped open an edamame and set the pod on his napkin before tossing the soy beans into his mouth like peanuts. Sara had always known her father ate fast, but for some reason, his chewing seemed extra loud and rapid now. She wondered if anybody else noticed it too. "So, Gene, what do you think about the Chargers' draft picks this year?"

Gene delicately placed an empty edamame pod on a plate next to him. He shook his head. "Honestly, I don't follow football." He shrugged.

Sara almost felt sorry for her dad. He was trying. The Chargers were like his religion. Discussing them with anyone was sacred. Couldn't Gene just lie and act like he thought the draft picks were exciting?

"So, I once heard that you can tell what kind of a person you are by how you eat sushi," Sara's dad said.

Tracy chimed in. "Yeah, some people take the warm towel and delicately wipe their hands and face. Then they fold it back up and place it next to their plate. They eat everything with chopsticks. Those people are organized and plan ahead. Others take the towel, quickly wipe down their hands, then set it in a small pile somewhere near their plate. They might eat their sushi with their hands. They're more laid-back, easy-going, messy."

Everyone listened as her dad continued to explain. "Tracy and I ate at a sushi restaurant in Hawaii when we were there last summer, and it had this whole list of all these little quirks and characteristics for people by how they eat their sushi."

Gene threw back his head and laughed. "How clever! That's hilarious. So the type of person who takes his towel, smears his dirty hands all over it, then throws it on his plate probably lives in squalor?"

"Exactly," Tracy and her father answered.

"Imagine the kind of person who doesn't use his towel," Sara's mother said. "What kind of person would that be?"

"An animal," Tracy answered. Everyone laughed.

After that, things were a little more relaxed. Gene had lots of recommendations for sushi, which provided for all kinds of yummy things to taste. Everyone at the table analyzed one another's sushi-eating habits. For the most part, they were all clean, organized, and the type who planned ahead. But maybe that was just because they knew they were under sushi scrutiny.

Only a couple of pieces of a spicy crab roll remained in the end. Allie and Sara swooped in and managed to stuff the remaining pieces somewhere inside their full stomachs.

The busboy had just cleared the plates, when the Japanese staff at the restaurant came bursting from the kitchen singing a Japanese version of "Happy Birthday." Sara felt her cheeks growing warm when she realized they were making a beeline straight for her. The ringleader held a bowl of green-tea ice cream with a candle sticking out of the top.

Sara's parents and their significant others sang in English, and Allie and Sara giggled sheepishly along.

"You didn't think we were leaving the restaurant without singing 'Happy Birthday,' did you?" her mother asked.

"I hadn't really thought about it." Sara took a spoonful of the creamy dessert, then passed it around the table. "Here. Everyone have some."

While they passed around the ice cream, Gene pulled a box from underneath his seat. It was wrapped in pink paper, with a big brown-and-pink polka-dot bow. She opened it up and found a leather planner. It was much more chic and sophisticated than the binder she'd been toting around everywhere. "Thank you," she said. "I love it, and I need it."

"That binder you've been carrying around everywhere makes you look like you're showing carpet samples or something. You needed something new, chief."

Allie gave her a bracelet she'd made using funky black and red cat's-eye beads. Tracy gave her a gift certificate to the best clothing boutique at the mall.

They were waiting for the check when her father slid a key across the table. She felt everyone staring at her.

"It's to the minivan," he said.

"Your dad and I talked"—her mother chimed in—"and we both felt it would be best if you put your money toward college when there is a perfectly reliable van you can drive. And once you go to college, you won't need a car anyway. Everything you'll need will be on campus. If you get good grades your freshman year of college, we'll help you buy a car."

She was a tiny bit disappointed. It was *her own* money that she'd saved, but their idea of driving the van made perfect sense. An education was far more important than a car. At least Allie and she would be matching. The minivan for the fertilizer plant wasn't quite as dilapidated as the Zebra, but it wasn't exactly the Honda Civic she'd had her eye on. She'd tried to envision putting some kind of wild patterned seat covers on the front seats and maybe a couple of bumper stickers of her favorite bands on the back windows.

"Let's go check it out," her dad said. "I had it detailed for you this morning."

"Thanks!" She forced a smile. "I mean, thanks for everything. You guys really are so generous." Did her response sound fake? Because she didn't want to be ungrateful. She had a car! Even if it was a van that had been used for hauling fish guts and cow manure.

They headed out to the parking lot.

"It's over this way," her father said.

"Where?" She didn't see the minivan anywhere. It took her a second before she noticed the gigantic red ribbon tied around a small silver Honda Civic. She screamed. "Is that for me?"

Her mother put her arm around her shoulders. "I thought you could use a little bonus for working as hard as you have this summer, so your father and I both pitched in a little more than we'd planned and bought you the car. You have been so professional, and mature. I'm so proud of you."

"Where did you get it?"

"From a young married couple, out of the *Auto Trader*. It has thirty thousand miles and it's immaculate. They took such good care of it. Wait till you see the inside."

She ran to the car and practically flung herself over the hood. "I love it! It's perfect!"

It was decided in the parking lot that Sara would follow Allie to her house, where they would drop off the Zebra. Then Sara and Allie were going for coffee. Really, Sara just wanted to drive around town in her new car.

After they ditched the Zebra, the first thing the girls did was roll down the windows, plug Allie's iPod into the cigarette lighter, and blast Angels and Airwaves.

Blake called to wish her a happy birthday, and Sara invited him to join them at Java Joe's. They stopped at a gas station for gum, then headed to the coffee shop. Sara had to parallel park, which was a little intimidating, but after a couple of tries and Allie's coaching, they squeezed into a spot.

They had barely set foot inside the coffee shop when Blake joined them.

He gave her a big hug before wishing her a happy birthday. "Let me buy your coffee," he said. "It's my birthday gift to you."

Sara got an iced mocha and Allie had the same. Blake had an espresso. They found a table and listened to Gorillaz blast from the speakers as they talked about cars and report cards. Blake's friend, Thomas, joined them. He was nineteen and worked at the catering business too. Sara knew him from some of the events. Thomas entertained them with stories of wild nights in Tijuana—one of the benefits of being over eighteen.

Neither Blake nor Thomas had a curfew, but Allie and Sara had to make it home by eleven. Blake and Thomas were headed for a party, and they walked with Allie and Sara to the car. Sara felt so independent and free as she went to unlock her car door. Her own keys. Her own car. It was surreal.

"Hey, I'm still taking you up on that movie," Blake said as they approached the Civic.

"Taking me up?" She laughed. "You're the one who came up with the idea in the first place."

"Well, whatever. You can drive us."

She shrugged, then smiled. "All right." For some strange reason, she suddenly felt sentimental toward him. They'd been working at these parties together for a long time, and there were certain things that only the two of them could understand.

As soon as Allie slammed the door behind her, she looked at Sara. "You're going to the movies with Slick?"

Sara shook her head. "He's been saying it for months. It'll never happen."

"I could see how some girls would like him," Allie said. "He's fun and cute."

They were both quiet for a moment.

Then Allie said, "He's nothing like Ian, though."

Sara felt her heart sink. "No. Nothing like Ian."

Twelve

"Hi, Ian. How are you? It's Sara." Allie's voice sounded confident as she spoke. She made it sound like calling Ian was going to be the easiest thing ever. "I was calling because I wanted to invite you to a party."

"Wait. Hold on," Sara said. "What if he doesn't even remember who I am? What if he knows, like, ten Saras? It's a pretty common name."

"He'll remember."

"Shouldn't I say something like, 'It's Sara Sullivan—I planned your CD-release party'?"

Allie shrugged. "You're being so ridiculous. But I guess if it makes you feel more comfortable."

Sara was picking at a chocolate-covered glazed doughnut. She'd been at Hole in the Wall Donuts for the past forty-five minutes, rehearsing what she would say to Ian.

She loved hanging out at the doughnut shop. It always smelled like coffee and freshly baked desserts. Allie let her try all the donuts she wanted. She couldn't understand why anyone would bother with bagels or muffins if they'd ever set foot in Hole in the Wall. They made the doughnuts twice the size of regular ones, and Allie's father had created his own secret recipe for the frosting and glaze. Sara had never found out what was in there, but she could eat ten frosted cake donuts in one sitting.

Most mornings, there was a line out the front door, and Sundays were wild. Sometimes people waited two hours for a doughnut. Allie tossed Sara an orange juice from the beverage fridge. "Here, have another. It's on the house."

"I hate this. All of this," Sara said. "It's so second grade. I mean, I haven't asked someone to go out with my friend, or whatever she is, since I was in junior high."

"Well, I already told you what I think you should do."

"I can't tell him the truth."

They rehearsed Sara's spiel at least a dozen more times until Sara felt confident enough to call him. "Okay, I'm ready," Sara said. "Can you turn the radio down a little?" The local rock station had been playing in the background. As soon as Allie lowered the volume, Sara dialed Ian. Her heart raced as the phone rang. Part of her hoped he would answer, and the other part hoped he wouldn't. She was dreading the conversation, but she also didn't feel like leaving a long-winded message on his voice mail or calling back. She just wanted to get it over with.

"Hello?"

He answered.

"Hey-er-Ian?" *Heyerlan?* Could she sound like a bigger idiot?

"Yeah?"

"Ian, it's Sara Sullivan. The one from the parties. The girl—"

"Yeah, I know. How are you? What's up? I didn't expect to hear from you."

"Well, me neither. I mean, I never really expected to call you like this. But, um, anyway, I'm calling because do you know Dakota London?" The words fell out of her mouth like popcorn. They seemed to scatter everywhere. All the rehearsing she'd done with Allie had gone straight out the window the moment she'd heard his voice.

"Tall blond girl?"

"Yes. Well, um, she's having a party, and she wanted to invite the band to come, or, I mean, you. But of course you can bring them if you want." She had no idea what she was talking about. "I guess she has a vintage fifty-seven Les Paul that her dad needs tuned. He won't be there or anything. In fact, her parents will be out of town. But she wants you to come and you can tune the guitar." This had "elementary school" written all over it.

She thought he would start asking a million questions about the guitar. Instead, he sounded confused. "Does she want us to play at this party?"

"Um, no." Sara realized that she was doing a horrible job of explaining. "She's just inviting you to the party. I'm kind of coordinating for her. And there is also going to be this guitar there that needs tuning."

Allie giggled in the background. Sara knew it was because the whole thing sounded so silly.

"I didn't know you were friends with her. Hmm. I wouldn't have thought you two would be friends."

She immediately began to analyze. Was it because he realized what complete opposites they were? Or was it because Dakota was so popular and wonderful that he couldn't imagine her being friends with Sara?

"Sure, I'll come tune the guitar, I guess. A fifty-seven Les Paul, you said?"

"Yes." She started to pace around the doughnut shop.

"That's a sweet guitar."

"It's a party. You don't have to come just to tune the guitar. You can bring the rest of the band, too. Or whatever friends you want."

"Okay."

She told him when it was.

"I doubt Tristan will go. He has poison oak all over his face, and he won't leave the house until it clears up. Jeremy is in Europe with his parents for two weeks, and Casey works in a cover band like I do. And I'm pretty sure he has a gig this weekend."

"Oh, okay."

"But I'll go," he said. "Only thing is, I don't have a car right now."

"I can give you a ride." Saying those words felt great. She felt so independent. She loved having a license.

"Right on."

It hadn't even been two seconds after she'd hung up before her phone rang. Dakota's words came out in rapid fire. "Did you talk to him? Is he coming? What did he say?"

"Yes, he's coming." Sara still walked from corner to corner.

"Did he say anything about me? Did he ask about me?"

"Um . . . he knew who you were."

"Wonderful! Now what will I wear?"

Allie was staring at her after Sara hung up. "You are way too nice. I can't believe you did that for her. I would've told her to—"

Sara took a seat across from Allie. "Please. I already know."

"Well, I think I can safely get out the beads now. It's noon." Allie turned the volume on the radio up and pulled out her stash of beads.

After twelve o'clock the doughnut shop became pretty slow. The occasional customer might stop by, saving themselves a trip for the following morning, but for the most part it was dead. Allie killed the afternoons by beading. Sara felt too fidgety to bead and instead watched Allie string together three rows of delicate red seed beads for a bracelet. As Sara admired Allie's work, she heard a familiar-sounding beat on the radio. The deejay's voice came over the sound of the music. "Here's a new one from one of our local artists, On the Verge."

Allie's mouth dropped open, and Sara clapped her hands together. "They're playing them on the radio!" Sara screamed.

"This is Nick Bones's station. This is totally because of the party the other night," Allie said.

"I can't wait to tell Ian." Then Sara thought about how she'd probably be driving Ian to Dakota's when she told him the news. She felt nothing but dread.

Thirteen

Sara wondered how long the excitement of slipping into a new car lasted. She looked forward to getting behind the wheel of the Civic more than small children look forward to Easter-egg hunts. She loved the car. Sometimes she would park in her driveway and wait a few seconds before getting out. She kept it cleaner than her bedroom and offered to drive almost everywhere she went with Allie.

She'd been a little nervous about picking Ian up. What if she got lost? Or worse, what if she got into a car accident with him in the car? However, when she slid behind the wheel of the Civic, she realized she might not be picking him up—period. Her nervous excitement quickly turned to worry when she realized that the car wouldn't start. She turned the key three times, and the engine didn't even crack. She dialed her father.

"Did you leave your cell phone charging? Or what about your iPod? Did you leave it in the cigarette lighter?"

"Oh." As the realization of what she'd done hit, she felt like a complete moron. She knew you couldn't leave things charging. She'd just been so flustered lately that she'd totally forgotten to pull her iPod out of the charger. She'd drained the battery. "I did," she said, ashamed.

Dad turned on his lecture voice. "You can't leave things charging in your car. Remember? We talked about this? You drained the battery. You're going to have to call the auto club and have them come jump it for you."

"I don't have my auto club card yet," she groaned. "It's on its way."

"Well, I can't come over there to jump your car right now. Tracy and I are already late for the Padres game. You're going to have to wait until tomorrow."

Mom and Gene were wine tasting and wouldn't be back for hours.

Part of her felt a little relieved. She had an excuse to get out of the whole event and abandon her unwanted matchmaking duties. It wasn't her fault that the car had broken down—well, it kinda was. But Dakota didn't have to know that. On the other hand, if she didn't go to the party tonight, Dakota would just reschedule. She'd only be prolonging her misery. She might as well just get it over with.

She called Allie. "I need a huge favor from you."

Allie listened while Sara explained her dilemma. "No worries. Shane's picking me up to go see that Owen Wilson movie. He should be here any minute. He can just pick me up at your place and the Zebra's all yours."

"Thanks! You are the best. I owe you big-time."

Sara heard the Zebra before she saw it coming. She'd recognize the rattling noise it made from anywhere. Before tonight, she'd never noticed exhaust streaming from its tailpipe though. A large gray cloud followed the Zebra like a shadow. The van screeched to a halt in Sara's driveway. "Here you go." The keys dangled from Allie's fingers as she climbed out of the driver's side.

"Oh, I forgot to tell you when you called. The AC broke. So you'll have to keep all the windows rolled down."

This was getting worse by the minute, but Sara didn't have time to complain. It was a ride, and without it she wouldn't be going anywhere. "Thank you so much." Sara didn't waste a minute and hopped into the driver's seat.

"You look great!" Allie called. She pointed to her neck. "And you're wearing the necklace again!"

Sara touched the blue beads. "Yeah, but just because I wanted to look cute." Maybe a small flicker of hope had still existed when she'd put on the necklace, but she felt ridiculous admitting that—even to Allie.

Allie rolled her eyes. "Whatever. Call me the second you get home."

Appearance wise, Sara had made a little more of an effort than her usual skinny jeans and tank top. She wore a strapless black baby-doll top that fell to her knees and a pair of destroyed jeans. The bright blue necklace popped from her neck. Maybe she did look great, but as long as she sat in the Zebra, she felt like her fresh appearance was getting sucked away with the wind.

She knew her makeup was starting to look oily. The wind whipped her hair around her head, and her clothes felt stuck to every square inch of her body. The twenty-five-minute drive to Ian's was plenty of time to make her look as though she'd just gone Jet Skiing in her own sweat.

His two-story house was in a typical suburban San Diego neighborhood. The band's van was parked in the driveway, and a couple of surfboards were propped next to the garage door. He surfed too? She'd been looking for someone to surf with for the past two summers.

Her stomach felt tangled up when she rang the doorbell. A brief moment of silence passed before she heard footsteps galloping down what she imagined was a staircase.

"I'm outta here." She heard his voice as the footsteps drew closer.

A woman called from somewhere far away. "What time will you be home?"

"I don't know!"

"Be careful. Call me if anyone gets drunk!"

The door flew open. "Hey." Those dimples never ceased to amaze her. He looked a little tanner, as if he'd been in the sun a lot since the last time she'd seen him. He held a hooded sweatshirt over his arm. She wondered what he thought when he saw her. He must be wondering if she'd jogged over to his house, she was so sweaty and disheveled.

"Sorry I'm so late" she said. "I had quite the fiasco when I was leaving." She told him about the dead battery in her car, then pointed to the Zebra. "I hope you don't mind a little heat. There's no AC."

"No worries. Our van doesn't have AC either. You should see the inside of it. I've made it a rule that if I drop something on the floor and it rolls under my seat, it stays under my seat. I'm afraid if I reach under there, something might bite me."

Sara laughed. "It can't be that bad."

"You have no idea. Five guys in a van can get pretty gnarly."

"Well, this car bites. I mean, literally. If you sit in the backseat, you may get attacked by one of the wires in the seat cushions."

His laughter was genuine. Only, the funny thing was, she wasn't kidding. She caught a whiff of his shampoo or soap. She wasn't sure which, but it smelled clean.

The Zebra was sweltering, and Ian threw his hoodie on the backseat.

"I almost forgot!" she said. "I heard you guys on the radio the other day. Right after I talked to you."

He nodded. "I heard us too, and lots of friends have said they heard also."

"That's so cool!"

"Yeah, thanks to the CD-release party. I don't think we'd be getting any airtime if it wasn't for our huge release party. Thanks again."

"My pleasure."

He told her about the band and how their tours were pretty small at this point, but they played in Los Angeles quite a bit. Now that the CD was out, they were getting more shows in Southern California for the summer. Once school started back up, he'd have to wait to play anywhere outside San Diego again. He told her stories from the road. She laughed hysterically when he told her how they'd once left a rest stop parking lot without Tristan. They made it ten miles before they realized.

"You guys are such opposites," she said.

"Yeah. I know."

The radio in the Zebra was broken. All

the windows were rolled down, so they wouldn't be able to hear the music anyway. Once they reached the freeway, the roar of wind kept the conversation limited. They had to yell just to understand a few words.

Showing up to Dakota's palace in the Zebra was like walking into prom wearing sweats and a T-shirt. The dilapidated car didn't really fit in with the massive canary palms and bubbling fountain in Dakota's yard. She wondered if the neighbors would call the police when they saw the Zebra.

Sara had totally forgotten that the passenger side door was busted until she was halfway around the car and she noticed that Ian was still inside. "Is there a trick to this?" he called. He fiddled with the door handle.

She rushed to the door. "Sorry, I have to let you out." It was kind of funny in a bizarre-first-date type of way—like she was the guy opening doors. His arm brushed hers when he slipped out, and it felt warm and sunkissed.

Dakota's house was like a hotel. Sara felt like the front door alone would swallow her. It would be so un-Dakota to answer the door. Sara figured she'd have to make some kind of remarkable entrance a half hour after everyone arrived. Her friend, Cassidy, let them in. Sara had sat next to her in biology last year. She seemed a lot nicer than Dakota.

"I'm so glad you came," she said to Sara. "I need to throw a party and I could use your advice."

Sara nodded. "Of course."

Dakota came down a massive winding staircase. She wore a long strapless sundress with a wild brown-and-red pattern on it, and she held a tiny white dog. Her hair was loosely thrown into a high ponytail.

"Hello, hello." She glanced out the window. "You brought Allie Bernstein's car? Where is your new car?"

"It broke down. Long story. Sorry we're late, by the way."

"No worries." Then she turned to Ian. He'd been quiet ever since they'd entered the castle.

"I'm so glad you made it! I can't wait to show you the guitar. Everyone is in the other room."

Approximately fifteen of Dakota's friends drank beer in a large room that looked like a French palace. Ornate gold and white woodwork covered the walls, and a huge crystal chandelier hung over the pool table. Massive

French doors opened to a large patio where a gigantic flat-screen television hung above a bonfire pit. Exquisite-looking patio furniture and a large black-bottomed pool with waterfalls took up the rest of the yard. A few empty beer bottles sat on the edge of the fire pit. Sara felt slightly underdressed around Dakota's friends. They all seemed like they'd stepped out of a dressing room with Nicole Richie's stylist. She had imagined an informal poolside barbecue and had dressed accordingly. All she could think was that Dakota's family had a flat-screen television outside? And inside? Two different shows were going on at once. She remembered what a big deal it was when her father had bought his first flat-screen TV, and it was half the size of *one* of Dakota's.

A couple of girls sitting near the pool whispered something about the guitarist from On the Verge being at the party. Sara was happy for his success, but she couldn't help but wonder what it would be like if his band wasn't played on local radio stations. Would they even care about him? Would Sara and Ian even be here?

She'd been too busy looking around to notice that Dakota and Ian had wandered off to a far corner of the game room. Aside from Cassidy, she didn't know a soul. She was about to head to the bathroom when Cassidy reappeared. "Hey, do you want a beer?"

Sara shook her head. "No thanks. I'm driving tonight."

"So you're the party planner?"

Sara nodded.

"Well, I'd like to throw a big party to get back at my ex-boyfriend. I'm sure you heard all about the drama that happened to me . . ."

Actually, Sara hadn't. Occasionally she got some juicy gossip from Allie, but for the most part, she was really out of the loop. She'd heard some time back that Cassidy had been dating an actor who made occasional appearances on some TV show. She wasn't even sure which show, and she'd never be able to identify the guy in a lineup.

Cassidy explained, "After the whole breakup, he ran off to St. Tropez with this girl who's an actress too. You may have heard of her. I want to have a huge party to get back at him. Maybe we could even call it a breakup party."

Sara wanted to listen to her, but her attention kept wandering back to Dakota and Ian. She couldn't help it. Her eyes were fixed on Cassidy, but her ears were perked toward Ian.

She tried to hear what he was saying. ". . . this guitar is amazing . . . an original . . . How long did you say your dad has had it? . . . Where did he find this?"

"I think he got it from an old roadie that worked for some really famous band in the sixties," Dakota said. "I couldn't tell you who. . . ."

How could lying come so easily for her? Sara wished she had the nerve to blow Dakota's cover. Instead, she kept her eyes on Cassidy, politely nodding and smiling while she shared her ideas for the party.

"Why don't we take it somewhere more quiet?" Dakota asked. "It's so loud in here . . . better to hear it upstairs."

She couldn't hear what Ian said, but she saw him from the corner of her eye. He carried the guitar as he followed Dakota from the room.

She wanted to groan out loud. That was it. They'd be doing rated-R things by nightfall. They'd be engaged by the sweet sixteen.

"So, I was thinking a weeknight might be kind of fun. Being summer and all. Everyone just wants to go to Mexico or LA on the weekends. What do you think?"

Sara realized that Cassidy was still talking to her. Her voice had become like white noise in the background. It took Sara a second to mentally hit rewind and try to figure out what Cassidy had just asked. "Oh, um, yeah, sure. I can check my schedule and get back to you on that one. But a weeknight should definitely work. We're actually booked a lot of weekends this summer anyway."

"Perfect. I really want it to be at the beach. Do you think we could do that?"

"I think so. As long as you don't want a band or anything."

"How much do you charge, anyway?" Cassidy smiled. "I forgot to even ask you."

It didn't really sound like something her mother needed to be involved in. Why not just do it for fun? Hang out with some people from school for a change.

"Well, maybe we can just plan it together. Just as something fun."

"Really?" Cassidy's eyes lit up.

"Sure."

She liked Cassidy. Cassidy seemed genuine and happy. Sara actually really liked the idea of a breakup party, too. Turning something negative into something fun was always worthwhile.

"Here's what I'm thinking. Just right off the bat," Sara said. "And you can tell me if you don't like my ideas."

Cassidy seemed excited as she waited for her to continue.

"I think we should play only upbeat breakup songs, like that new one by Fergie. Nothing depressing or slow. Then we should have a big bonfire pit—oh that just made me think of something else. We shouldn't even call it a breakup party. We should call it a move-into-the-future party or a new beginnings party, and everyone will have to throw something from their past into the bonfire. Because, I mean, do you really want your ex to think that you care about the breakup that much?"

Cassidy shook her head. "No."

"If he finds out that you're having a breakup party over him, he'll probably just be flattered. It might be best not to even let him know you're thinking about him. Do we even want guys at this party? I'm thinking it might be nice to have a girls' night. And it doesn't even have to be specifically about breakups. Some people might want to throw clothes from their old crappy jobs into the fire."

"I love all this!" Cassidy clapped her hands. "This is all fantastic! I'm so excited. When can we start planning?"

"Call me this week."

They discussed the party for a few more minutes before Cassidy went to greet a new arrival at the front door. Sara thought of Ian and Dakota upstairs and felt her heart sink. She was surprised by the pain and tried to tell herself that she really had no right to be annoyed or sad if he was hitting it off with Dakota.

She made a mental list of reasons as to why she needed to get over it and be happy for Dakota and Ian.

1. Ian was an acquaintance. Nothing more. It's not like there had ever been anything between them, except for a few good conversations at events they'd worked together. He had every right to like Dakota.
2. And why wouldn't he like Dakota? He had no idea that she was a spoiled, manipulative, guitar-bidding nutcase. He'd only seen her pretty, fun side.

Sara knew one thing for certain. This was the last time she was helping Dakota with Ian. And it wasn't because her feelings for Ian came into the mix. It was because she didn't want to feel used again. This wasn't part of the sweet-sixteen party plan. As she sat on Dakota's game-room couch, she felt like she'd just been a means to an end. Sara had been a way for Dakota to get Ian to her house.

Sara sat on the couch for a few minutes, trying to figure out ways to make it look like she'd chosen to be sitting on the couch by herself. She scrolled through her text messages and was happy to see Allie in her inbox.

Hows it going?
Xo,
Allie

Sara thought of all that she wanted to write back. I feel really used. Ian and Dakota seem to be hitting it off. I wish you were here, or better yet, I wish we were hanging out anywhere but here. Cassidy is planning a move-into-the-future party, and I feel like it really applies to my life right now as well.

However, she kept it short. While she wanted to look busy, she also didn't want to look like the weird chick who was obsessed with text messaging all night. At some point she was going to have to socialize. She was "the party girl." It shouldn't be that hard.

Im never doing this again.
Sara

Ian and Dakota reappeared forty-five minutes later. Sara didn't think it was a good sign that they were laughing. She'd kept busy by playing pool with three guys she'd just met. They were now playing doubles, and she'd teamed up with a tall guy named Marco who went to a different school. Her team was winning, and Sara had sensed surprise from her new teammate when he realized that she was pretty good with a pool cue. She was on her third Diet Coke and wondered how long it was going to take her to come down from her caffeine high. She felt wired, which only resulted in more anxiety over the whole Dakota and Ian situation.

Even though Ian still held the guitar,

she hoped he was going to say that he was ready to go home. However, something about the guitar made him magnetic. Everyone in the room had requests for him.

Ian barely had a chance to wave to Sara before he was thrust into the opposite corner of the room to jam with Dakota and her friends.

Sara and Marco won the pool game, and as soon as it was over, she headed for the bathroom. Her bladder felt as though it were going to burst from all the Diet Coke. The bathroom that adjoined the game room was bigger than her bedroom at home. The ceiling seemed headed for heaven, and her footsteps echoed every time she moved.

She took a moment to primp in the mirror. She'd left her blush and lip gloss in the Zebra, and she wished she had it now. The moist beach air made her look washed out. She'd watched *Gone with the Wind* in her history class when they were studying the Civil War, and she thought she remembered Scarlett O'Hara pinching her cheeks to make them brighter. She went ahead and gave each cheek a few pinches. When she opened the bathroom door, Dakota was waiting.

"Did you fall in the toilet or something?" She laughed.

Sara was surprised by the question. "No."

"You were in there forever. Why are your cheeks so red? What were you doing in there?" She raised her eyebrows.

"Nothing. I was just—"

Dakota squeezed her arm. "Things are going great with Ian," she whispered through a gritty smile. "I totally think he's in for the party."

Sara tried to conceal her disappointment. "That's great. So you asked him?"

"Well, no. But I will. I can tell he'll come though. He's been flirting with me all night. He told me he'd teach me to play the guitar if I wanted."

"Really? I mean, wonderful."

She was about to walk away when Dakota grabbed her arm. "Wait. I have to talk to you about something else."

What did she want now?

"So, when are my parents surprising me with the car? I mean, at what point in the party can I expect the car to roll up? I just want to be prepared to put on my best surprised face."

Sara was speechless. Dakota knew about the car?

"I'm not really sure I know what you're talking about. What car?"

"Oh quit. Please. I know my mom called you. My little sister has been spying for me for months now. All I have to do is take her to the mall with me and my friends every other week, and she'll hide under my mom's bed and listen to everything she talks about. I know I'm getting the car. I just don't know when."

"Honestly, we really haven't decided on when." It wasn't a lie.

"Well, I want it to show up early in the party. Like maybe that should kick off the party. I want to be able to drive it in front of everyone."

"The decision isn't really up to me," Sara said.

A sly smile crinkled Dakota's eyebrows. "If you ever need anything forged, let me know. I have the best report-card guy," she whispered.

"Yeah, how'd you do it?" Sara couldn't help her curiosity.

"You know that dweeb, Glen Oldsmund?"

Sara vaguely remembered a skinny guy with thick glasses and *Lord of the Rings* stickers covering his binder.

"He's one of those straight-A people and apparently a whiz with forgery. Don't ask me how he does it, but the whole thing cost less than my last pair of jeans. And don't tell anyone."

"I won't."

When she returned to the game room, her teammate was waiting for her. Another pool game was in the forecast. Since they'd won, they were up to play the next pair. This time it was Cassidy and another girl from school, Brittany. Most of the party had drifted over to Ian's half of the room. Sara made the shot, then glanced at her watch. She had to be home by midnight. It was ten thirty. That meant the latest they could leave was in a half hour.

As she finished her game, she listened to Ian take requests in the background. Someone would ask him to play a song, and he'd be able to just strum it out, without sheet music or anything. If he couldn't remember a song, then he asked them to hum it for a second so he could refresh his memory. His talent amazed Sara, and she hoped that Dakota appreciated all his wonderful qualities.

Sara also hoped that he would get tired of playing before she had to interrupt. The last thing she wanted to do was be the big geek with the curfew who interrupted the jam session. Luckily, he made eye contact with her. "You ready?" he asked.

"Yeah, sorry to break up the music, but I have to get home."

It was hard to miss the annoyance that flashed in Dakota's eyes, and Sara wondered if anyone else had noticed it.

"I can give you a ride," Dakota said to Ian. "I mean, if you don't want to leave with her right now."

Ian thought for a moment. Was he mentally whipping up an excuse to get out of there? Or was he wondering how he was going to politely tell Sara that he didn't need a ride home? Sara felt like everyone was staring at her, like she was the only dork with a curfew and a shady minivan in the driveway. The sudden sound of light rain seemed to engulf her, and at the same time, her neck felt much lighter. In a nanosecond everyone in the room pointed to her. It seemed like slow motion as she watched her summer of love necklace come down like sleet from her neck. Blue beads scattered in every direction. The sound of Dakota's laughter muffled out the rapid fire of beads pinging against table legs and the floor. For the first time that night, she wished her cheeks wouldn't turn rosy. Her face felt hot, and she knew she was turning three shades of crimson.

"My necklace," was all she could think to say. She went from embarrassment to annoyance to sadness almost as quickly as the necklace had snapped. The timing couldn't have been worse. And it's not like she'd provoked it. She'd just been standing there, motionless. It shouldn't have been that embarrassing, but Dakota's laughter made it worse, and the smirks from her friends were nerve-wracking. Sara forced herself to laugh too, even though she wanted to disappear. For a moment she felt like tears were imminent, but she suppressed the urge to cry. She had to keep it cool.

The only people who displayed any

signs of empathy were Ian and Cassidy. Ian looked disappointed. "That's a bust," he said. I bet we can pick them all up though. I'll help you." He leaned over and started collecting beads from the floor.

Sara dove down next to him, immediately scooping up the beads. "That's okay. Really. I can do it. You can just go on playing the guitar if you want." She was babbling now, which only added to her shame.

Cassidy joined them on the floor. "I'm sorry your necklace broke, sweetie. It was cute, too."

"It's okay."

It seemed like it took forever for the three of them to pick up all the beads. Sara delivered them to a nearby trashcan. "You sure you don't want to save those?" Ian asked.

"Positive." As if she was ever going to make another necklace as long as she lived. The next necklace she made would probably break while she was taking her diploma at graduation. This couldn't be a bigger omen. Her summer of love necklace had shattered in front of Ian and Dakota. How symbolic was that? Cosmic forces had sent her a huge sign, and it wasn't in her favor.

"I promised I would be at the studio early in the morning, so I should probably head out." He handed the guitar to Dakota. "Tell your dad it plays great."

"I'll walk you guys out." Dakota's tone was chipper, but Sara knew that underneath it all, she was fuming. She wondered if Dakota had asked him to go to the party. If so, what was his response?

The temperature outside was much cooler since they'd arrived, and Sara wrapped her arms around her chest as they walked to the Zebra.

"Thanks again," Ian said.

"Don't forget to mark my party on your calendar."

So *she'd done it*. She'd asked him.

He nodded. "I just have to double-check that we don't have a gig that night."

The car ride home was a little different than the car ride there. It was cooler and all the windows were rolled up. So the silence in the van provided for lots of conversation. Even though they both never seemed to be at a loss for words, Sara couldn't help but be slightly preoccupied with his response to Dakota. She tried to forget about it, but really she was just dying to know if he wanted to go to Dakota's party, or if he was just being polite.

He told her all about his family. Like her, his parents were divorced. His mother and father had both remarried and subsequently had more children. Ian and Tristan were the oldest. They also had twin brothers on his dad's side who were only three years old.

"They're so cool," he said. "And total opposites. Just like Tristan and me. One is really wild. The other is really introverted and quiet. But they're both really cool."

"So just one sister?"

"Yes. She's six years younger than me. What about you?"

"It's just me. You know, my parents are divorced. Neither one has more kids. My mom's dating the florist, Gene. I'm sure you've seen him around at events."

"Really? Your mom's dating Gene?"

"I know, it's kind of a shocker."

"Well, no . . . I just didn't know. Gene's cool. He was asking about my guitar the other night. He actually knows a lot about guitars."

"Gene knows about everything. He always has something to talk about."

"He used to play in this really cool band back in the eighties. They never made it big, but they had a pretty big following in Southern California. They were called The Weeds."

"What? Now I'm really shocked. What kind of music was it?"

"Rock."

"Gene? In a rock band?"

He nodded.

"I don't believe it."

"I swear. You should ask him about it sometime."

She left the car running when they pulled up to his house. The glow of a street lamp filtered through the windshield of the Zebra. "Thanks for picking me up," he said.

"Sure."

He leaned over to open his door and she almost forgot about the busted handle. "I have to let you out," she said.

"Oh, yeah."

She turned off the ignition, then walked to his side of the car. She smelled his clean scent as he climbed out. An arm's length stood between them. She noticed the shadow of a cat dart from beneath a car on the opposite side of the street. "Thanks again," he said.

"No problem."

For a moment, the only sound was the light fizz of his neighbor's sprinklers.

She spoke first. "Well, have a good rest of your weekend."

"All right. Talk to you soon."

She quickly headed back to her side of the van, feeling as though this might go down as the weirdest night of her life, PG of course.

Fourteen

Four torturous days went by when Sara
didn't know whether Ian was coming to
Dakota's sweet sixteen. The answer came
from Cassidy. She'd called to discuss her
"new beginnings" party.

Leah's kitchen remodel had begun, and
about half a dozen construction workers
were demolishing the current room. Sara
closed the door to the office so she could
hear Cassidy better.

"So, I have so many girls who are into
this party. You have no idea. The only one
who thinks it's dumb is Dakota. In fact, I
don't even think she'll come."

Sara's heart sang. A Dakota-free party

sounded great. A saw shrieked in the kitchen, and what Cassidy said next was muffled.

"Ever since"—*BUZZZZZSHCEEER!*—"Ian"—*BZZSHEEEEEER!*—"her date at her sweet sixteen, she's been on cloud nine."

"I'm sorry. I didn't hear what you just said."

"Oh, I was just saying that ever since Ian asked Dakota out, she's been on cloud nine."

Despite her disappointment Sara pretended to be happy for her. "Oh, I didn't know. That's good. They should have fun together."

"You haven't heard? Yeah, I guess he's going to be her date at the sweet sixteen. I'm surprised you didn't know. She wants him to ride in her limo to the aquatics center. She's, like, totally in love now."

Sara faked a chuckle even though her heart felt as though it were being torn to shreds. Dakota had spent weeks composing her "limo list." Only an elite few had the privilege of riding from the aquatics center to the reception hall in Dakota's special limo. Now, Ian would be one of them. She felt her stomach turn.

"Yeah, so anyway, for those of us who

aren't in love, we'll have so much fun at my party!" Cassidy declared.

"Yeah, for those of us who aren't in love," Sara mumbled. If Cassidy only knew the truth.

It was a low moment. Sara's better judgment was telling her to listen to what Allie had said. If Ian wanted to hang out with Dakota, then something was wrong with him. He was a crazy idiot. Or, he was truly blinded by her. If he was that big of an idiot then she shouldn't be sad. But she couldn't help it if she was disappointed. She'd really hoped that there was more to him—that he would have said no to Dakota. Deep down, she knew he wasn't a crazy idiot. The whole thing came as a complete shock. She'd really been hoping he would've used the *band has a gig that weekend* excuse.

She did her best to focus on Cassidy's party plans. For the duration of the conversation, she told herself that she needed a new beginnings party too. She needed to forget about Ian. She brainstormed all kinds of ideas for the event. Topless waiters were the only boys allowed. Since they were on a budget, Sara thought it would be fun to serve only finger foods, and ones that required peeling a layer off and chucking something into the trash. It was consistent with breaking up and moving forward. Things like peanuts and shrimp.

After she hung up with Cassidy, her phone beeped, indicating a new message. She played her voice mail.

"Hi, Sara. It's Dakota." The sound of her voice immediately made Sara nervous. "I just want you to know that I'd like my ice sculpture to be pink ice. Oh, I'm not mad about my wet suit anymore. My mother found a special company that can make me a custom wet suit. It's going to have a V-neck, so I can show a little cleavage, and the shorts are going to be very Daisy Duke. They're also sewing on a special cape with my initials in bright gold lettering and 'sixteen' written beneath them. Oh, and count Ian in. He's definitely coming." *Beep.*

She flipped her phone shut. That was it. She mentioned Ian like he was some kind of afterthought. Did she even care about him? Or was he just an accessory to her?

She spent a few minutes staring into

space, mindlessly tapping a pen on the edge of the desk in the office. Ian had asked Dakota out. It didn't help that the construction workers were blasting a boom box down the hall, and the current song blaring from the speakers was by On the Verge.

"What are you thinking about?" Her mother's voice came from the doorway.

Sara sat up and closed the leather planner Gene had given her for her birthday. "Oh, nothing."

Her mother watched her. "You don't look like you're thinking about *nothing*. What's up?"

Sara used the breakup party as a cover up and described all of her ideas for the event. Her mother's laughter was loud. "That is one of the best party ideas I've ever heard of! You're so creative, Sara." She shook her head. "So much more creative than me."

"Well, it wasn't exactly my idea. It was *her* idea to have the breakup party. I've just filled in the blanks."

"I'm really proud of you," her mother said. "You've gone above and beyond my expectations and you'll be putting me out of business by the time you're twenty." She sat down across from Sara. "And I'm really proud of you for the way you've handled the London event. You've shown a lot of maturity. I know it hasn't been easy for you."

If she only knew.

Fifteen

Sara had known that the Kenny Street Band would be playing at the Hayes/Casper wedding for several months, so it was no surprise when she arrived at the reception hall and Ian was setting up with the band. She waited for a jolt of sadness to course through her veins or a moment of total of disappointment to seize hold of her emotions as a result of just looking at him. She was relieved when she didn't feel anything. Nothing. Zilch. All of Allie's pep talks had really helped. She could accept the fact that he was probably dating Dakota. He, like everyone else, was blinded by her charm.

She hadn't realized she'd been staring at him when he looked up from whatever he was doing with an extension cord and smiled at her. Rather than feeling total sadness, she felt herself grow warm from the inside out. She was still completely attracted to him. She couldn't help it. His forearms looked so strong and sinewy, and the way his curls fell over his forehead made her want to be closer to him. As she waved back, she decided that feeling attracted to him was worse than feeling sad. She didn't want to like him anymore. She needed an Ian detox. Somehow, she had to get him out her system. She hadn't expected him to hop off the stage and head right over to her.

"Hey," he said. "I figured I'd see you tonight."

She remained cool. "How are you?"

"Good." He nodded. "Really good."

She couldn't help but wonder how much time he'd been spending with Dakota, and if his new romance contributed to his feeling *really good*.

"You have time to walk to the soda machine with me?"

She glanced at her watch. "Yeah, okay."

They headed to the patio of the beach resort. "I think I saw a machine near the parking lot when we got here."

It was a perfect summer day. It was one of the rare events they'd planned that took place during daylight hours. The air wasn't too soggy, as it sometimes gets near the coast. Rather, it was warm. Waves crashed as the tide danced over the sand.

"So, did you hear that we were in *Rush*?"

She gasped. "No! Nick Bones reviewed the album?"

He nodded. "Yeah, and it was a really good review."

"Ian! That's great news. You guys must be so happy. I'm so happy for you."

He nodded. "Yeah, things are going really well." He smiled. "In all areas of my life."

That must include his love life. What had Dakota done to him?

They found the soda machine, and Ian asked her what she wanted.

She began to pull her wallet from her pocket, but Ian was already depositing coins into the slot.

She thanked him for the Sprite before he bought himself a Dr. Pepper. They headed down a wooden bridge back to the reception hall. She was dying to ask him about Dakota but thought she would sound too nosy.

"Oh, I almost forgot," he said. "I have something for you."

"For me?" Sara watched while he dug inside his pants pocket, wondering what it could be. Was Dakota now sending party instructions with her date? She expected him to produce a long list of requests in Dakota's handwriting.

Dangling between his fingers was a necklace of small blue beads. He held it out for her. "I saw this in the mall the other day when I was buying my mom a birthday present. I couldn't remember exactly what yours looked like, but I thought this seemed similar."

Utterly shocked, Sara paused before taking the necklace. A whirlwind of emotions took over. He was giving her a necklace? Talk about signs. Her summer of love necklace had broken and now the guy she liked had replaced it. How symbolic was that? But then she had a major reality check. He was going to the party with Dakota. He couldn't like both of them. He was just being nice because he felt sorry for her that her necklace had broken in front of a crowd of twenty. The gift had been out of sympathy, nothing more. "That is so sweet of you. You really didn't have to do that." She shook her head.

"It was nothing. I just saw it and thought you should have another one. It kinda sucks that your other one broke."

"Thank you." She lifted her arms, then held the two ends of the necklace at the nape of her neck.

"It looks good." He nodded. "Here, let me help you." Slowly, she turned her back to him. She felt the light brush of his hands on the back of her neck as he picked up the clasp. She held up her hair so it wasn't in his way. Her heart raced when she felt his fingertips against her skin as he grappled with the clasp. His hands felt like they belonged on a guy. They were a little rough, but in a sexy way. After he finished, he squeezed her shoulders and turned her around to face him.

"How does it look?" she asked.

He nodded. "Looks great."

She wondered what Dakota would think if she knew he'd bought her a necklace. She felt guilty for taking it. Was this inappropriate? Taking gifts from her client's date? "Thank you," she said. "But you know, you really shouldn't have." For a moment, she debated giving it back. But she didn't want to be rude, either.

He shrugged. "It was just a small gesture

to thank you for all that you've done for my band. We wanted to do something for you right after the party, but everyone kind of got wrapped up with summer. So, here's my thanks."

Knowing it was just in gratitude for what she'd done made her feel less guilty. "I think that's one of the most thoughtful things a client has ever done for me. I mean, I don't think I've ever received such a nice thank-you gift."

He shrugged. "It wasn't a big deal."

Her mother's voice crackled into her headset as they reached the reception hall. "Sara, have you seen the guest book? I can't find it anywhere."

She was tempted to reach up and turn off her headset. She was tired of a party need interfering with the things that she wanted. What she really wanted to do was finish her soda with Ian. She looked at him. "My mom's in my ear. So I think I have to go."

"Yeah, sure. I'll see you later," he said.

She scurried off.

Sara passed Gene on her way back to the reception hall. He carried a centerpiece that covered his entire torso and chin. "Love that necklace. Is that new?" he asked.

Sara touched her neck. "Yes."

"You're blushing," he said.

She quickly took her hand away from the necklace. "No I'm not."

The rest of the afternoon went by fast. As Sara watched the lady in white, she couldn't help but touch the beads on her neck every ten seconds. It had become a subconscious thing. Half the time, she didn't even realize that she was doing it. Every time she walked past a mirror, she stole glimpses of the necklace. She'd never received a gift from a guy before, even if it was just replacing something she'd already had. She couldn't believe how strange it was that he'd replaced the very necklace that had been symbolic of him. The cosmic forces were fooling with her. She totally believed in signs, and the ones she was getting were so confusing.

Before she knew it, the bride and groom were on their way to the airport for their Caribbean honeymoon, and the band had packed up. She was packing up candles when she noticed Ian headed her way. "Hey, are you hungry?" he asked. "I have to go to the studio later, but I was going to grab a bite before I went down there." He'd taken his tie off and loosened his collar. He still wore his black slacks. His Converse peeked from beneath them. The shoes looked a little tattered next to his band-issued pants.

Her mother and Gene were standing a few feet away and seemed preoccupied with the wedding favors they were packing up. Guests always forgot their favors, and Sara and her mother always packed them up and saved them for the bride and groom. In this case they were Godiva chocolates.

She felt her stomach growl. "Starving."

"I was going to head to Luigi's in Mission Beach. You know, the restaurant near the roller coaster?"

She nodded. "Yeah." She'd eaten there with Allie once. Her first instinct was to say no. She wanted out of her suit and pumps, and she had a headache. "Okay," she said. She was still curious about what was going on between Dakota and him. Maybe she could find out some info.

From the corner of her eye, she caught her mother and Gene staring. When she glanced at them, they quickly looked away.

They walked to the restaurant from the reception hall. The noise from the roller coaster was energetic, and in a strange way refreshing. The sound of the wheels rolling over the tracks followed by adrenaline-laced screams seemed free. Summer nights at the beach were always lively, and many of the shops on Mission Boulevard were lit up. She wrapped her arms around her shoulders. Even though it was summer, the ocean breeze was chilly.

"Are you cold?" he asked.

"I'm okay."

"Here. You can have my hoodie." He draped it over her shoulders, and she instantly caught a whiff of his clean shower scent—something she was starting to become well-acquainted with. She could probably detect the scent in an outhouse.

"Thanks."

Did he have to be nice on top of cute? This would all be so much easier if he was a jerk. Was she doing the right thing by being here with him? Or was she just prolonging her misery? Deep down, she knew that the smart thing to do was to forget about him.

They sat on the patio, and they both ordered calzones. She asked for broccoli and pineapple in hers. Instead of gagging with disgust, Ian asked for a bite.

"I wouldn't have guessed that yours tasted good, but that's a great combo," he said, nodding.

His was bursting with pepperoni, and he offered her a few pieces too.

Afterward, they walked past the roller coaster and ended up on the boardwalk. The occasional guy on a skateboard or group of drunk college students rambled past them, but for the most part the boardwalk was empty and dark. The only visible sign of the ocean was the foamy white crests of waves that moved like phantoms on the black horizon. They found a place to perch themselves on the edge of the beach wall. Her toes barely touched the ground, and the front of his shoes were buried beneath the sand. "How are you ever going to get all that sand out of your shoes?" she asked.

He shrugged. "Good question."

They both cracked up when they looked at his feet. A brief moment of silence followed before Ian's eyes locked on hers. For a moment she wondered if she had something on her face. She hadn't expected him to lean toward her. His lips meeting hers happened quickly, but gently. He tasted warm and smooth. His kiss felt like the soft glow of a candle, drawing her in. Every nerve in her body seemed to melt, and she suddenly felt an urge to feel more of him. Somewhere inside her, she had this gnawing sense that what she was doing was wrong, but she didn't let it stop her. She just wanted more of that warm, soft feeling.

"Bossy" shattered the moment like a bullet, and she suddenly realized why she'd had that gnawing sense that something was wrong. Making out with her client's date? It couldn't get any worse. She pulled away from him first.

"Who's that?" He chuckled. "Your mom?"

Obviously, her mother seemed a little bossy. But that came as no surprise. She was the head honcho at almost every event Ian had been to. "Er . . . uh . . . no . . . it's just a client." One that happens to be your date. And she happens to be madly in love with you. A client whose entire state of happiness hinges on whether this party goes over well. And right now, one of the biggest ingredients in her happiness is you.

"That's funny."

"What?"

He pointed to her phone. "That you have that song programmed for a client."

"Oh, yeah." She tried to chuckle.

"Now come back here," he said affectionately as he leaned closer. She was dying to kiss him again. *Dying*. It felt so perfect, and he was so warm. She could stay there with him forever. Instead, she jumped from the wall and grabbed her backpack. Her heart was racing. This was all happening way too fast. She'd just made out with the guy she'd had a crush on all summer, who also happened to be the biggest and most demanding client's date to the biggest event of her life. Aside from being totally unprofessional, she couldn't imagine the devastation that could result from what she'd just done. What if Dakota found out? What if her mother found out? What if *anyone* found out?

"Um, I think I better head home." she said. "I have to get up early tomorrow, and . . . well, it's late."

"It's barely eight." He slid off the wall. "Is everything okay?"

"Um . . . yeah."

Her mind raced. How was she going to fix this? Her heart was dying to fall into his warm embrace again, but she couldn't. Her head was screaming for her to stop. She had to think of business first. She had to blow him off, convince him that Dakota was the right girl for him. He was going to the party with her. He'd even committed to it himself. And what was that all about? Maybe he was a jerk? Was he off kissing Dakota too? What the hell was he doing? Two-timing both of them?

"Listen, I know that you and Dakota have this whole thing planned for her party . . ."

He looked puzzled, but she continued talking. "And the last thing I want to do is get in the middle of that. Do you think it's really fair after the commitment you've made to her to be doing this? I think it's best that we totally forget about what just happened, okay?"

An ocean breeze blew his bangs over his forehead. "What do you mean?"

"I mean, you're going to Dakota's party with her, and if she found out about this, it would be . . . catastrophic . . . to, well, everything. I'm the party planner. Not the party pooper." She knew she sounded like such a dork, and she wished she could take back all her words.

"Yeah, I'm going to Dakota's party. But I'm not going *with* her."

"Yes, you are."

"Who told you that?"

"Everyone. You're her date. Aren't you?"

He shook his head. "Not that I'm aware of. Look, she asked me to come to her party. The only reason I said yes was because I thought you were going to be there."

Her heart skipped a beat.

"Really?" She almost leaned in and kissed him again. "I mean . . . you have to be her date. She thinks you're her date. She thinks you're going with her."

"I don't have to do anything. And I don't want to go to Dakota's party with her. She's weird."

She felt torn between jumping for joy and running for dear life. She felt her heart sinking to her knees. She was thrilled that he didn't like Dakota, but he wasn't supposed to like her. At least not now.

"Look, I like you," he said. "But I'm starting to get this weird feeling that you're just using me to go to some party so you can keep Dakota happy."

"No. That's not the case! I swear!"

"Then what is it? Because I can't figure out what's going on here."

Sara didn't have an answer. What was she

supposed to say? I like you too. But can you please put those feelings on hold until after August, when Dakota's party is over and my mom's kitchen is finished? Can you please dress in island castaway clothes for one night, ride in a limo with San Diego's most annoying sixteen-year-old, then profess your feelings for me? As she tried to think of something to say, he shook his head.

"Call me whenever you have an answer." With that, he turned around and walked away.

"Ian, wait!" The sound of the crashing waves muffled her voice, and he disappeared into the dark night. She held on to his hoodie. "You forgot your hoodie," she called. He didn't come back.

Sixteen

"This is so cool!" Allie screamed into the phone. "You're so scandalous."

"But I don't want to be scandalous!" Sara said. "I should've never gone to the beach with him. But how was I supposed to know that he was going to kiss me?"

"Gee, let's think about this for a minute. First, he buys your soda, then he buys you a *necklace*!" Her voice became louder with each sentence. "Then he basically takes you on a date!" She practically screamed the words. "What did you want him to do? Sing out his love to you onstage?"

It was midnight. She still hadn't even taken her nightly bath. She hadn't even changed out of her clothes from the wedding that afternoon. She looked at his hoodie lying on her bed. Figaro was already curled up on the hood. "Cassidy told me that he was going to the party with Dakota. She was on cloud nine, blah, blah, blah. He was riding in the limo. I mean, for a minute there, I thought he was playing both of us."

"Well, obviously he's not."

"Yeah, I know that now." She groaned. "Why does the first guy who has ever kissed me have to be wrapped up with her?" She thought for a moment. "There's only one thing left to do."

"Good. Call him and apologize. Screw Dakota and go on a double date with Shane and me!" Allie howled.

"No. Actually, that's not what I was thinking. I have to call and tell him to go to the party with Dakota. This can't fall apart now. I can't steal her date. I'm supposed to be making her party the best party ever! Not the worst! I mean, I've never even heard of anything like this happening. Ever. What kind of party planner am I? I'm like a party planner from *Days of Our Lives*. It's like a soap opera."

Allie laughed. "It's kind of funny."

Sara shook her head. "It's so not funny.

careers. How will my mother and I ever get hired to do another sweet sixteen if rumor has it that the party planner's daughter steals the birthday girls' dates?"

Allie laughed. "I think it's hysterical."

"Thanks." Sara's voice was flat.

Allie quit laughing for a moment. "C'mon. Listen to yourself."

"What?"

"You're not begging him to go to the party with her. I don't think he's gonna go anyway at this point. I would consider Dakota and Ian a lost cause."

Sara thought for a moment. The whole ordeal was draining her, and she just wanted to go to bed. It had been such a long day. Ian giving her the necklace seemed like it had happened a decade ago. She could hear Gene and her mom splashing downstairs, and she wanted to tell them to keep it down.

"Even if I did call Ian and apologize, and I'm just saying if, because I'm not going to, I think he would hate me at this point. He totally opened up to me, and I told him he had to go on a date with another girl. I feel like such an idiot. I *am* an idiot!"

"No, you're not. Listen. The guy really

likes you. Do you think one little misunder-standing is going to suddenly squash all his feelings? Ian will get past it if you clear the air *soon*. Sara, you have the rest of your life to plan the best parties ever. But you're only going to meet a guy like Ian once. Does it really matter what happens with Dakota's party? I hate to see you walk away from such a great guy for one party. Find Dakota a different date."

Sara took a deep breath. Inside, she felt that Allie might be right, but her head was telling her that Allie was completely wrong. And she couldn't get that kiss out her mind. She'd dreamed about finding a guy like Ian, and now he was here. All the time she'd spent worrying about bad breath and teeth collisions, and then her kiss with Ian felt so natural. She longed for more. Was it pos-sible that her first kiss would be her only kiss? She didn't know what to do.

Seventeen

Flames smoldered in the beach air. Sara watched as Cassidy sang along with Destiny's Child's "Survivor" before dumping a very expensive-looking leather jacket into the bonfire. "Screw boyfriends!" she screeched.

Several girls cheered as flames popped like fireworks and sent off sparks over the sand. Another girl, Amanda Finely, twirled toward the smoke, then launched a size 14 dress into the pit. She'd taken up running over the summer and had recently lost eight pounds. Following her was Ashley, the girl Tristan had hooked up with the night of the CD-release party. Sara watched as On the Verge's CD flew into the flames like a

Frisbee, then as the CD cover melted like molten lava inside the inferno.

Seeing the CD made Sara's heart ache. Was it symbolic? Was it some kind of fateful message? Was fate telling her that any kind of a relationship with Ian had turned to ashes? As much as she'd tried, Sara couldn't feed from the crowd's energy.

She was barefoot, and the sand felt grainy and cool between her toes. Her hair felt as unruly as brussels sprouts in the moist ocean air. The only boys at the party were five guys they'd hired from their rival high school's wrestling team to serve drinks topless. Jocks weren't Sara's type, but she couldn't ignore their flawless bodies. Chiseled, tan chests above rough, worn blue jeans came with each soda.

She thought about throwing the blue necklace into the pit but quickly dismissed the idea. The bottom line was that she missed Ian. She'd replayed their kiss over and over in her mind a million times. She thought of his smile and the way he'd gently put the necklace around her neck so many times that she'd practically remembered these moments to death. She didn't want to watch anything associated with him burn.

She wanted to see him. She wanted to hear his voice and his laughter and eat calzones at Luigi's. In fact, she'd be willing to go anywhere with him if it meant that she could see him again. She'd called him twice, but he hadn't answered or called her back. Who could blame him? She'd acted like a jerk. At this point, the damage had been done.

Cassidy popped in next to Sara and threw her arm over her shoulder. "This party is perfect! I think we should do this every weekend!" Then she whispered gruffly in Sara's ear. "I'm in love with the topless waiter named Brett. The one over there, serving Chelsea and Candace right now." She squealed, "I totally think I'm going to ask him to Dakota's party. She said I could bring a date." Then she squeezed Sara's arm so hard that Sara was sure there would be a bruise tomorrow. She whispered in her ear again, but the music was so loud that she practically had to scream. Sara thought she'd be deaf, too.

"Oh, and I almost forgot. Ben, the waiter with the blond hair, asked about you! We should all go on a date! They're so cute. Ohmigod, that would be so fun!"

Sara smiled. "Yeah, that would be fun."

She was only being polite. Really, she was just thinking that Ben was nothing like Ian. She tried to bury her longing for Ian. She should be having fun. It was the first time Sara had actually felt a little like a guest instead of an assistant. Besides hiring the waiters and helping Cassidy purchase drinks, there hadn't been a ton of work. Better yet, she didn't have to play superhero at this party. No debutante or birthday girl needed to be rescued from some catastrophe. All these girls were pulling themselves out of catastrophes. Anything could go wrong and it wouldn't matter.

Cassidy elbowed her. "What's wrong with you anyway? You just don't seem like you."

She was the last person Sara could confide in. Anything Sara said would probably go straight back to Dakota. "Nothing. I'm just sorta tired."

"Ohmigod! I love this song!" Cassidy began to jump up and down as Gwen Stefani came blasting from the speakers. She tugged on Sara's hand. "C'mon, let's go dance. We have to dance to this one."

Sara didn't have much of a choice as Cassidy dragged her toward a group of girls who were already well into the dance moves.

"I'm not a very good dancer!" Sara yelled over the music, but Cassidy didn't hear her. Cassidy fell into a groove as she lifted her arms and swayed her hips in sync with the beat. Sara felt self-conscious, but the music was pounding and somehow she began to move her body. At first her hips felt as stiff as knives and her feet felt like bricks as she struggled to keep up with the beat. Once she forgot about what everyone else thought, she began to move freely. And who cared what they thought, anyway? She was having fun. It felt good to move to the music and to hear the other girls' hollers and catcalls coming down around her like rain. For most of her life, she'd been standing on the sidelines.

Gwen Stefani finished and another upbeat song came on. There were absolutely no sad or sappy love songs allowed at this party. Each song that came on was fast paced and danceworthy. Before Sara knew it, song after song flew by. She felt like she could dance all night. She danced until she was out of breath and the back of her tank top felt damp. She finally understood why it was so hard to peel people off dance floors at the end of parties. Dancing was a blast. She wanted to go to parties like this every day. It was the first time in days that she'd taken a hiatus from thinking about Dakota and Ian.

"I'm gonna grab a soda!" she yelled to Cassidy over the music. "You want one?"

"Sure, I'll come with you."

They were heading to a topless soda god when Sara thought she heard the subtle sound of buzzing heading in her direction. She turned to Cassidy. "Do you hear that?"

Just as she said the words, she watched as one of Cassidy's friends, Samantha, came skidding over the sand on the kind of scooter that the driver stands on. Sand flew like spray paint behind the back wheels. Sara knew who it belonged to. The scooter belonged to Samantha's ex-boyfriend, Travis. Sara knew this because Travis lived two houses down from Sara and had driven the entire neighborhood insane with the scooter's whizzing high-pitched motor. She was just shocked that the scooter could stay balanced on the sand.

Sara hoped to God Samantha didn't have plans to burn the scooter. It was like slow motion as she watched Samantha jump from the machine, raise it above her shoulders like a sumo wrestler might, and heave it into the fire.

"That has GAS-O-LINE!" Sara screamed. "EVERYBODY BACK!"

Her warning was followed by an ear-splitting pop and a fireball bigger than an elephant.

"Whoooa!" A nearby waiter watched in awe.

"I think my eyebrows are singed," a distant voice whined.

Sara immediately scanned the area, looking for burn victims. Fortunately, no one needed to stop, drop, and roll. However, the entire east side of the bonfire looked as if they'd just come from a coal mine. She watched as the guests pointed to one another and laughed.

Sara turned to Cassidy. "I'll be back. I have wipes in my car." Baby wipes were part of Sara's emergency kit.

She'd just set off for her car when she felt her cell phone vibrate against her thigh. She'd tucked the phone deeply into her jeans pocket. She pulled her phone from her pocket and read the text message.

WE NEED TO TALK ASAP. CALL ME.
DAKOTA

Did she know? She had to know. Was this another one of her little games? The message seemed so un-Dakota. In the past few weeks, Dakota had sent her lists of demands and concerns before insisting that Sara and Leah address all of them before calling her back. Even though it was all in writing, her tone seemed abrupt. What was with the capitals? It looked like she was yelling.

Rather than calling Dakota back, Sara hurried to her car. She climbed into the front seat, closed the door behind her, and dialed Allie. The music from the party sounded distant while she waited for Allie to pick up.

Pick up, Allie. C'mon, pick up, please.

"Hey, girlie, how's the party going?"

"Thank God you answered. Dakota knows. She totally knows." Sara read the text message verbatim.

"That doesn't mean she knows. How would she know? Do you really think Ian told her?"

Sara thought for a moment. "No. But

what if he told someone else, who then told her?"

"Guys don't do that. They just don't. They're a completely different breed. I mean, we, of course, would tell each other everything, but guys don't kiss and tell."

"I guess you're right. Who else knows besides you, Ian, and I?"

"Call her back, then call me back."

She hung up with Allie. Sara's heart pounded as she dialed Dakota's number. Even though Allie's thinking made sense, she was still nervous.

Dakota answered on the first ring. "Hey." Her voice sounded flat. Another very bad sign. The Dakota that Sara knew usually sounded wired and bubbly.

"What's up?" Sara asked, trying to sound casual.

"Promise you won't tell anyone?"

"Yes, of course."

"Ian's not calling me back. In fact, I don't even know if he's going to the party with me."

"He's not?" Sara tried to sound surprised.

"Well, the thing is, he said he would come to the party, but I never really asked him if he would come with me. I just thought I would save that until we got closer to the party. I didn't want to scare him away. But I've already told all my friends that he's going with me."

Sara actually felt kind of bad for her. She sounded so sad, and Sara didn't want to see anyone suffer humiliation. Not to mention, she felt like this was all her fault. "So do you think you can call him?" Dakota asked.

Sara should've seen the question coming, but, as usual with things involving Dakota, it made her feel like she'd just been hit from behind by a train. "Um . . . well, I'll try. I think they're getting ready to go on tour. Maybe that's why he's not calling. Maybe he knows he won't be in town." She hated lying, and she knew that by doing so she was only making the situation worse. If Dakota found out about what had happened, Sara was not only going to be the bitch who stole the birthday girl's date, but a total liar on top of it. But what could she say? *Sorry, Dakota, he doesn't like you. He told me after we finished making out.*

"Have you thought about asking someone else to the party?" The question felt deceitful coming from Sara's mouth.

"No. And I can't have a shameful legacy

following me to my party. What will every-one think when they find out the guy I told them I was going with isn't coming after all? I have to take a backup date? Who does that? A desperate loser is the only type of person I know who will end up in that kind of situation. Not me."

Sara felt like telling her that she shouldn't have lied to everyone, but that definitely wasn't going to help anything. Worse, it seemed like the whole party was just one big game for Dakota, and taking Ian was only about winning in Dakota's mind. Did she really even like him, or did she just want to take him because she didn't want to be "a loser"? The thing that drove Sara crazy was that she wasn't playing any games. Sara genuinely liked Ian. It wasn't some dumb party game for her. It was love.

"Call him. You're the party planner, and he's part of the plans."

"I'll see what I can do." As soon as she finished saying the words, she realized that she was speaking to deaf ears. Dakota had already hung up.

Sara pulled out her emergency kit and headed back to the party to go clean up another mess.

Eighteen

Sara and her mother were sitting in the living room, going over all the details for Dakota's party. Though Sara had done a decent job of keeping up with all the major details, there were still all the small, yet very important details her mother was good at remembering. Dakota wanted an ice sculpture, and since the party was in August, they were going to have to make sure they used a sculptor who had refrigerated transportation. Ice sculptures were made using a special mold that kept the water crystal clear when it froze. It was an ordeal to keep the water clear and sparkly, so Leah wanted to make sure that they gave the artist plenty of time to prepare.

"She wants her sculpture to be pink," Sara said.

Leah shook her head. "No. I've seen dyed ones. Tell her the beauty of the sculpture comes from the clear ice. We can provide pink lighting that will look beautiful. You'll have to explain all this to her."

Sara took notes.

Leah also wanted to make sure the sculptor could provide transportation to remove the remaining block of ice after the party, because Dakota's massive self-portrait statue could flood the entire reception patio once it melted.

They talked about the food. There would three stations of food at the party. One was a full Japanese sushi bar. The other was going to be a fruit and smoothie station. And the last would be a nacho buffet with every kind of topping one could think of.

Gene's company was going to make five hundred plumeria leis for the guests. The cost alone was enough to buy a small car. They needed to designate spots for the exotic birds. The list went on and on.

Leah's notebook was wide open, and Sara noticed an upcoming wedding in

August. The Kenny Street Band was penciled in with all the other vendors. Unless Ian had quit working for the cover band, he would be there. They'd be forced to cross paths. She worried about what Ian was going to do when he saw her. Or worse, what he wasn't going to do. Would he completely ignore her?

"Bossy" came blaring from Sara's backpack.

Her mother chuckled. "Dakota. That makes me laugh. Can I get you to put 'Barracuda' on my phone for that woman who handles all the tablecloths?"

In spite of the fact that her heart was pounding from the mere sound of Dakota's ring, she managed to laugh. "Sure, I'll show you how to do it."

Sara's phone was tucked in the small pocket inside her backpack, which was beneath the coffee table separating Sara from her mother. Even though the phone was buried, the song still sounded as clear as if it were sitting right out in the open. They both eyed her backpack before Sara continued talking. "So anyway, back to the party."

"You're not going to answer it?" Her mother looked puzzled.

Sara had tried to ignore the phone but apparently her mother wasn't getting the drift. "I'll talk to her later," she mumbled. "I have to meet Blake for the movies, and she'll keep me on the phone forever." The last thing she needed was for her mother to find out about any of this. Not only would Sara be banned from her mother's party-planning business, but she'd be thoroughly embarrassed. Her mother would be morti-fied if she knew that Sara had kissed a client's date—even though Ian had techni-cally never been Dakota's date.

"The London party is next weekend. It might be something important," her mother urged.

"I'll call her later. I can't reach my back-pack."

"Well, here. I can. I'll get it for you. I'll talk to her."

"No!" Sara hadn't meant to shout.

Her mother shot her a look.

Sara tried to sound calm when she spoke. "I mean, it's probably best if I talk to her . . . since it's been mostly me anyway."

"Just tell me where it is."

"It's . . . in . . . the . . . pocket."

She watched her mother unzip the outside pocket, which was the wrong one. Sara hesitated before correcting the mistake. She sort of hoped it would go to voice mail by the time her mother found the phone. She'd been avoiding Dakota for two solid days. Never in her life had she avoided a client, but she couldn't help it.

Her mother's fingertips had barely touched the phone when it quit ringing. "Oh well, you missed it," Sara said. "She'll call back later. Anyway, back to work."

No sooner had she spoken the words than "Bossy" came piercing from her mother's lap. This time there was no excuse.

Her mother held up the phone.

"Hi, Dakota. It's Leah! Sara and I are doing a little switcheroo. She's taking notes right now, and I'm taking calls today. We're actually going over your party." Her mother laughed. "Uh-huh . . . yeah . . . what's going on?"

Sara's heart pounded. She heard bits and pieces of small talk, and it was hard to tell exactly what they were discussing. It sounded mostly like ice sculpture stuff. Her mother gently talked her out of using dyed ice.

When she was finished, she held out the phone for Sara.

She had no choice but to answer. "Dakota, hi. How are you? I've been so swamped and I've been meaning to call you back—"

"Did you call him yet?"

"Um . . . er . . . I tried but—"

"Do you know something I don't know?"

"Er . . . no . . . I—"

"You totally know something I don't know. What do you know? Tell me. Did you hear something? Did he say something to you? You know something, don't you?"

Dakota had become a paranoid monster. The irony of it all was that Dakota's worries weren't that unrealistic. Sara knew a lot. She knew that the chances of Ian coming to the party were about as great as snow in San Diego. She knew that she had called Ian—twice as a matter of fact. And it hadn't been on Dakota's behalf. It had been to apologize for acting like a complete idiot at the beach the other night after he kissed her.

"Listen, I think we need to remember that he has an extremely busy schedule. He's not the type of guy who's going to be sitting around playing video games or hanging out with friends. He works a lot. I'm sure he'll call me back as soon as he has a chance."

It wasn't a total lie.

"What am I going to do?"

Sara squirmed in her seat. "Um . . . I'll be happy to help you find another date. . . ." Sara's voice trailed off. Were those tears that she heard? Was Dakota crying?

"This is horrible," she wept. "This is going to be the worst party ever." This wasn't the first girl to have a complete and total meltdown before her big day. Sara had heard enough birthday girls declare through a teary haze that their sixteenth birthday party would be the worst day of their lives. However, this usually involved some kind of problem with their gown or the band. The last time she'd witnessed a major meltdown was last summer, when they'd planned a sweet sixteen that involved several topless male models holding white tigers on leashes. The models and the tigers were supposed to accompany the birthday girl when she arrived at the party in her Egyptian gown and headpiece. It was a grand entrance meant for a goddess. However, it became a grand entrance for Old MacDonald when goats arrived instead of tigers. The birthday girl had a full-blown meltdown when the farm animals began leaving a trail of blueberry-like poop all over the red carpet.

At least, the goat/tiger mix-up hadn't been Sara's fault. Never had she ever heard of a party planner stealing anyone's date. Never.

"It's not going to be the worst party. It's going to be the best party ever. Please, there is really no need to cry. I promise everything will work out."

"You promise you'll talk to Ian?"

Sara paused. She couldn't lie. She also couldn't bring herself to talk to Ian on Dakota's behalf. Her mind raced. What should she say? "I'll . . ."

Suddenly Dakota's weeping stopped. A hollow silence filled her earpiece. It was a miracle. The call had been dropped. Things like this never happened to her. Usually calls were dropped during a critical moment of one of Allie's stories—not when she needed an escape route more than ever.

She flipped the phone shut, then turned it off. She didn't care if she missed important phone calls from other clients. She couldn't answer the phone again with her mom anywhere in the vicinity. The curious looks she'd been getting from her mom's side of the table were making her squirm.

"What's going on?" her mom asked. The inquisition was inevitable. Sara knew it was only a matter of seconds before she started getting pounded with questions. "She was crying?"

Sara nodded, wishing her mother would, just for once, decide not to be nosy. "It's a long story," Sara said, hoping this would stop the prodding.

Somehow, her mother always had a way of getting things out of her. It didn't take long before Sara was pouring out the entire debacle of Dakota and Ian to her mother. Strangely, it felt good to tell someone. Sure, she had Allie. But Sara was starting to wonder if Allie was getting sick of talking about it. Besides, Allie had already shared her strong opinions about how Sara should handle the situation. It was sort of nice to unload on a fresh set of ears.

"There. There it is. That's what's going on," she said as she finished the story. "And I know it's all my fault. And the last thing I want to do is hurt the business or ruin the kitchen remodel." A long silence followed. Sara spoke just to fill the air. "So I guess I haven't been doing as good a job as you thought I was. I probably don't even deserve my car."

She didn't know what to expect from her mother. Sara fidgeted with her pen as she waited for her mother to say something.

"Honey, I'm sorry." She watched her mother wipe away a tear. Okay, totally not the reaction she expected. What's worse, she didn't want her mother to cry. She'd only seen her mother cry when her grandpa died, and a couple of times during the divorce. This was serious. Her mother was always in control. If her mother cried, that meant that everything was really out of control. Mothers weren't supposed to cry.

"Mom, please don't cry. Really, please. I'll fix everything," she said slowly.

"I feel like this is my fault." Her mother took a deep breath. "I shouldn't have let you take on the responsibility of this party. When you told me you didn't want to do this, I should've listened to you." Within a couple of seconds, her mother pulled herself together. She took a deep breath as the tears subsided. Then she seemed so serious and concerned. "This past summer, you've really demonstrated how responsible you are and how well you can handle things on your own." She looked sad as she spoke. "I feel like we're a team. You're a young woman now."

"Really?"

Her mother laughed, and Sara was glad to see her lighten up.

Sara chuckled too. "I mean, oh. I guess I am. I just never thought of things that way."

"You are. You're growing. You're going to go off to college in a couple of years. And I think I made a big mistake by making you feel that we had to put the business first in spite of our feelings. Those aren't the priorities that I want you to have. I just want you to be happy. And I haven't always put the business first. I was being a hypocrite."

"You were?"

Her mother nodded her head. "Yes. Look at Gene. He is one of the biggest vendors that we use. Imagine if things went badly with him, and we had to cross paths at a million more weddings. I mean, things won't go badly, but my point is that I still put my personal feelings first in that situation. Listen, I don't care what happens with this Dakota London party. Why don't you just tell her that I have you working on other events now, and I'm taking over from this point on? If she finds out about Ian, well then that's just too bad for her. She needs a lesson or two herself. I don't care if she's mad at us. You have to do what's important for you. Honey, it's important that we make these parties special, but not at the cost of our personal lives."

Sara thought for a moment. This had been the most she'd talked to her mother in the PG days, and she was glad she'd had the chance to finally sit down with her and discuss non-party-planning things.

She glanced at her watch. She had to pick up Blake in ten minutes. "Mom, I appreciate the offer, but I'm going to finish what I started. I'm older now and I really think I can handle this myself. Somehow I'll fix this situation, but backing out now isn't the way I want to do it."

The August heat had drawn a crowd to the movies. It seemed everyone was eager to escape the triple digits and head to a dark, air-conditioned theater. When Blake had called her that morning to go to the movies, she'd been reluctant. However, sitting around dwelling on all her problems was going to drive her crazy. And what better escape than the movies?

Sara and Blake bought tickets to the latest Owen Wilson comedy. Blake had offered to pay, but Sara insisted on buying her own ticket. She didn't want him to get the wrong idea.

Blake took a place in line for cold drinks while Sara went to the restroom. The bathroom buzzed with girls. Sara took a moment to check her messages while she waited in line. She'd sort of become obsessed with checking her messages, hoping that Ian would call her back, then feeling crushed when her messages were all from Dakota and Allie. She had no messages. After she used the restroom, she primped in the mirror, then headed back to find Blake.

She'd just left the ladies' room, when she thought she heard her name. She spun around and faced Ian. He leaned against the wall next to the men's room. "Ian. Hi," she said slowly. "How are you?"

"Good. Just waiting for Tristan. He's in the bathroom. How 'bout you?"

"I'm fine," she said, even though she was dying inside. She wanted to tell him she'd be a lot better if they could just talk about everything. She wanted to tell him that she'd been a complete idiot. "I have your hoodie in my car," she said. The words had just popped from her mouth. It was all she could think of. In a strange way, she'd been reluctant to give the hoodie back, because it was the only connection she had left to him.

He nodded. "Oh, cool. Thanks. I'll get it from you at the next event."

So he had no plans to ever see her outside of work again? She'd been hoping he'd say something like, *Cool, we should go out for coffee anyway so we can talk and make up and I'll get it from you then.* That's when she knew it was really over. He really didn't care about hearing what she had to say.

They looked at each other for a moment. She wanted to feel his warm arms around her again, to feel the glow that had come from their kiss. "Sara," he said. "I guess we—"

"Hey, dude," Blake said as he approached. He held two sodas and a big tub of popcorn to share.

"Oh, hey. What's up?" Ian looked at Blake, then at Sara.

If Blake had waited just two more seconds . . . She was dying to know what Ian was going to say. Furthermore, now it looked like Blake and she were on a date.

"Nothin' man, just going to the movies. How about you?" Blake said.

"We're actually on our way out."

"And we're actually just friends," Sara blurted out. "Blake and me." Oh, God, why had she said that? Ian and Blake looked truly puzzled, and she felt like a complete jackass.

Tristan emerged from the bathroom wearing sunglasses. Ian headed toward his brother. "Well, you guys, enjoy your movie. Take care."

Sara watched him walk away. She felt glued to the spot.

"You all right?" Blake asked.

"Oh, yeah." She looked at Blake. "Fine." He handed her a large Sprite as they headed to the theater. She suddenly wished she hadn't gone to the movies with Blake. She felt weird and uncomfortable, and she just wanted to run to the parking lot and talk to Ian.

"What's wrong?" Blake asked.

"Nothing, really. It's fine."

"Do you and Ian have a thing going? I mean, that seemed really weird back there."

"No. Nothing is going on."

She was a bad liar, and after they found

seats, Blake managed to pry some information from her. She told him only that she'd kissed Ian once, then said something stupid and now everything was ruined. She kept all the details of Dakota to herself.

"This is why I don't want a serious love life," Blake said before he threw a handful of popcorn into his mouth.

She laughed. "Really deep, Blake."

He shrugged. "I just want someone I can party with and hang out with and who doesn't want to get too serious. I just want to have fun."

"That's so romantic of you." She chuckled, feeling slightly relieved that he probably didn't view their outing as a date.

Then an idea so perfect hit her, she was almost annoyed with herself for not thinking of it sooner. She was such an idiot. The solution was simple.

"Blake, what are you doing August twenty-fourth?"

"I might have to work, but you know, I can always flake out if I don't want to be there."

"I have a party I'd like you to help out with."

Nineteen

Blake and Dakota were perfect for each other. They were like the male and female version of each other. Setting them up seemed like a no-brainer, and Sara was surprised she hadn't thought of it sooner.

However, the matchmaking process would have to be handled delicately. Blake and Dakota went to different high schools, so they'd never met, which was a good thing. She wanted Blake to appear new and intriguing. Sara knew she couldn't come right out and suggest that Dakota take Blake to the party as her date. She'd have to introduce them to one another, and she had to make Blake appear desirable.

So she came up with what she thought was the perfect plan. Blake, like Sara, wanted to branch out as a caterer someday and handle his own projects. Leah had helped the Londons pick out a caterer, and it wasn't Blake's father. Sara couldn't tell Dakota to get rid of her caterer. Instead, she planned to tell Dakota that Blake was the hottest up-and-coming caterer in town, and he'd be willing to look at Dakota's menu plan free of charge and offer any suggestions. He'd be like a menu consultant. He'd be there to make sure they had only the best food at the party. Fingers crossed, sparks would fly.

In a normal party situation Sara would never ask anyone outside the vendor they were using to advise on a menu. But this wasn't a normal situation, and she needed to get the two of them in the same room. Dakota wouldn't know any better. Sara would be able to convince her that she needed Blake's advice. As far as Blake went, Sara had convinced him that advising Dakota on her menu would only add to his experience as a one-man act.

The meeting was held at the same Starbucks where Dakota and Sara had first met. Sara felt nervous as she entered the coffee shop. Criminal memories came to mind, and Sara half expected to see posters of Dakota, the male models, and her posted on the walls, banning them from ever entering the coffee shop again.

If her idea didn't go as planned, she would be left with only one option. She'd have to come clean. Telling Dakota the truth about Ian meant that all hell would break loose. Sara imagined lawsuits and the business going down in a blaze of scandal. Her mother would have to find another line of work, and Sara might be able to get a job at Hole in the Wall Donuts. She'd already gone over all possible tragic outcomes with Allie, who'd tried to assure her that none of the above would happen.

A total shocker, Dakota arrived on time. Perhaps her punctuality was due to the fact that she'd brought her mother. Sara hadn't expected Mrs. London, and her presence created a problem. How were sparks supposed to fly between Dakota and Blake when Dakota's mom was there? How could any kind of romance occur with a parent around? Not to mention, Mrs. London was a little intimidating. This might be a little weird for Blake.

"Hi, Sara," Mrs. London said. "Dakota and I thought it would be best if I came along since there are so many last-minute things that need to be discussed. And she said that you were meeting someone to discuss the menu? We're really happy with our menu. I don't know who this person is, but he's not part of the catering company we hired. So if there are any changes to the menu, I'd like to know about them."

Sara felt her plan crumbling and tried to keep it together. This was an ambush she hadn't expected. She played it cool. "Of course! I'm glad you came along, Mrs. London. You have wonderful taste, so your opinion in everything we choose will be very valuable. Every detail is important. My mother and I want you both to feel completely happy."

Mrs. London produced a flattered smile. "Well, you know I have hosted several functions."

Sara smiled back. "I know. I'm sure they were all beautiful."

Now she just hoped that Blake held up well. She'd made him sound like an expert to Dakota. Mrs. London's presence had already put a damper on the mood. Dakota was quiet and hadn't even bothered with her spontaneous little coffee game. Instead, she ordered a bottle of water and sulked from her side of the table.

Techno beat like a dinosaur's heartbeat in the parking lot. Sara knew this meant that Blake had arrived. She glanced out the window and, sure enough, there he was—windows down in the Escalade. An elbow hung over the driver's side of the car. She watched him park. Dark sunglasses perched over his nose. He was all bling-bling with his large platinum chain and the oversized diamond-studded *B* that dangled on his chest.

"Now, tell me what's going on with this boy?" Sylvie said.

Sara took her gaze away from the window. "Blake? He's great. He's going to make this menu perfect. I'm surprised he could even make it today. With his busy schedule and all the dates he has. He's so—"

"No, I mean the one who Dakota wants to take to the party."

"She's talking about Ian," Dakota interjected. "What's going on with Ian?"

"It's all she can think about," Sylvie said. "The party is a week away. We just want to know if he's coming or not."

"Hey, ladies," Blake said as he slid into his seat.

Blake's arrival at the table couldn't have come at a better moment. He pulled off his shades when he glanced at Dakota.

Blake reached in to shake Dakota's hand, and she barely lifted it. Sylvie managed to produce a curt smile.

Sara reached into her planner for the London-event menu. "Here, Blake." Sara passed it to him. "Have a look."

Silence hung over the table like a heavy tarp. Sara fiddled with a spoon she'd used to stir her mocha latte while Blake looked over the menu. Dakota continued to sulk, and Sylvie glanced at her watch three times. "So, here's what I suggest," Blake said. "The appetizers you have on here are all vegetarian. You should start off with some shrimp cocktail and perhaps chicken skewers as well. That's very island and beach themed. Variety is really key in party menus, and not everyone is going to want . . ."

Dakota flipped open her phone to check the time. When she snapped it shut, Blake glanced at her. "I would also suggest having fruit for dessert instead of mousse."

"But mousse is my favorite," Dakota said.

"And I'm a vegetarian," Sylvie chimed in.

Blake looked bewildered, and Sara didn't blame him. She suddenly felt terrible for dragging Blake into this. She'd made it sound like menu consulting would be a blast. He'd hardly been with them for five minutes, and the Londons were already hacking into him like a planted pine tree before Christmas.

"I think what Blake is trying to say is that not everyone is going to want to eat only vegetarian." Sara attempted to mediate. "He's just looking out for the best interests of your guests." As Sara explained, she heard a very familiar sound. It was On the Verge. It wasn't even the radio. Someone who worked at the coffee shop had decided to put on the CD.

She watched Dakota's eyes go from surprise to torture. She turned to her mother. "This is Ian's band."

Mrs. London's eyes zoomed in on Sara. "Sara, have you tried to call him?"

"I have." It wasn't a lie.

"Well, then, what's going on?" Sylvie held both hands out. "This not knowing is making my daughter crazy."

"Look, I'm sorry to break this to you,

but he's not coming. All right?" Sara was surprised by her own tone. She'd never known she was capable of snapping, and she hadn't planned on breaking the news to Dakota like this.

"What?" Dakota started to cry. "Why not?"

Sara took a deep breath. Maintain composure. Don't say anything you'll regret. She hardly noticed the sound of Mrs. London's cell phone ringing.

"Excuse me, I have to take this," Mrs. London said. "It's my husband." She plugged one ear with her finger as she held the phone up to her other ear.

"I can't believe you!" Dakota said. "You're totally out to get me. Just like everyone else!"

"Dakota, I wanted to tell you before. But I thought maybe there was hope to resolve the situation. But he just can't come. I know you're disappointed. And I wish there was more I could do."

She caught a glimpse of Blake from the corner of her eye. He looked positively startled. Sylvie looked pissed, and Sara wondered what she was telling Mr. London on the phone. Was she telling him to cancel his check to the party planners?

Because her expression indicated total dis-
pleasure.

"What did you do?" Dakota wailed.
"Things were going great between me and
Ian. What did you say to him? I know
you've had your eyes on him this whole
time. You're just a backstabber."

Sara's jaw dropped. Now she was angry.
"What? I've done nothing but try to help
you. And if he doesn't like you, that's not
my fault! I didn't say anything to him, or
provoke him in any way. In fact, I've put my
feelings for him on hold for you!" she
roared.

"So it's true! You do have feelings for
him." She turned to her mother. "I told you
she was stabbing me in the back."

Sylvie was too engrossed in her phone
call to notice Dakota.

"Screw this," Blake said. "You people are
nuts." He scooted away from the table, then
beelined from the coffee shop.

This wasn't how things were supposed
to go. And as she turned back to face a
dismal-looking daughter-and-mother duo,
Sara realized that she was out of ideas.

Mrs. London closed her phone. The
expression on her face was frightening. Sara

had an urge to jump from her seat and follow Blake out the door, but she couldn't run away.

Mrs. London's eyes darted over Sara, then found Dakota. "I just got off the phone with your father. And you have some explaining to do."

Dakota sat up. "What?"

"Apparently, the school's called. Does the name Glen Oldsmund ring a bell?"

Sara knew who it was. He'd forged Dakota's report card. Suddenly, Sara felt nailed to her seat. She wouldn't miss this for the world. Dakota was so busted.

Dakota shook her head. "Glen Oldsmund? He's such a dork. I have no idea who that is."

"Well, apparently he knows you very well. Your name was at the top of the forgery journal that he kept."

Mrs. London looked at Sara. "I'm sorry we wasted your time today, Sara. But Dakota is in deep trouble. I'm not even sure if she'll be having a sweet sixteen. The school's talking about suspending her for the entire first semester next year." She turned to her daughter. "They want to send you to Jenson High."

Jenson High was where the really bad

kids went. Kids who got into drugs or gangs. Dakota at Jensen? It didn't get juicier than this.

Dakota began to sob. "What? You're canceling my party? But I didn't do anything! I swear!"

Several people inside the coffee shop stared. Sara thought about how different things were from the first day they'd met at Starbucks. Dakota seemed like she'd owned the place back then. Now she looked childlike, with her blotchy red face and her desperate tears.

Mrs. London stood up. "Come on, we have to go home. Your father is furious. I told him we'd be there in twenty minutes."

"But I didn't do anything! I swear!"

Sylvie looked at Sara. "We'll be in touch."

Sara watched them walk all the way to their car. There was nothing she could do to save the day at this point.

Twenty

Sara wasn't surprised that the party was still on. Common sense had told her that Dakota would somehow get the party and the car and probably a load of attention from all her forgery schemes and scandals. Mrs. London had called Leah the day after the whole coffee shop blowout and said they'd already spent too much money—all nonrefundable—on the party, so they didn't want to cancel. She'd also explained that Dakota was going to need a car to drive herself to her new high school a half hour away, so she was still getting the Mercedes, too. Sara could only chuckle to herself when she thought of Dakota pulling up to a school rampant with gang members and druggies in her new luxury car.

Dakota's story about getting transferred to Jensen for a semester had made headlines in the local paper. This was mostly because her parents were fighting the school district to keep her at Bay Side High School, and all of Dakota's buddies had started a petition to keep her around. There had even been a protest outside of the head of the school district's office.

Surprisingly, through it all, Dakota had seemed to forget about Ian. It was like she had bigger fish to fry now. Sara, however, had not forgotten. She still missed him. She wondered if she would ever be able to forgive herself.

She'd been thinking a lot about what Allie had said. She had the rest of her life to be an event planner. But she was only going to find a guy like Ian once. Maybe it was time to focus on other things. As she set up for Dakota's party, she reflected on her summer. So many things had happened.

First, she'd gotten her driver's license and a car. Then her first kiss, and it had been with a really great guy. She'd spent a lot of time with people her age this summer. There had been a debutante ball, the CD-release party, the new beginnings party, and, of course, Dakota's sweet sixteen. It had been fun hanging out with Cassidy and her friends, and, of course, Ian.

The morning of the party went by quickly, as preparations always did. Sara blew through her list of tasks. Dakota's parents had chartered several luxury buses to transport five hundred guests to the aquatics center. Earlier that morning Sara and Leah had spent an hour stocking the plush buses with candy and sodas for the guests. They'd stayed up until two in the morning wrapping segments of sea-weathered rope around T-shirts that read *Dakota's Sweet Sixteen*. Each guest would leave the party with a T-shirt.

Sara could hear the buses pulling in, then the buzz of voices. Before long, Sara was helping Dakota climb into her custom-made wet suit.

"How do I look?" Dakota asked.

Even in underwater gear, she still managed to look like a runway model. "Beautiful."

"Hey, Sara?"

"Yeah?" Sara was looking at her clipboard when she answered.

"Thanks for everything."

"You're welcome." It was the first time Dakota had ever said thank you, and Sara sensed that Dakota really meant it. Sara smiled at her, then continued to look at her list.

1. Dakota's grand entrance.
2. Dakota gets her car.
3. Dakota leaves with male-model chauffeur in her new car.

Dakota continued, "You know, I'm not mad about Ian. I never really liked Ian anyway. He's not my type. And my father says I should never trust a traveling musician. He's probably better for someone like you."

Sara smiled to herself. Whatever Dakota wanted to believe was fine by her. She looked up from her clipboard. "Good. I'm glad."

Dakota grinned mischievously. "But I have another favor to ask you. And I think you owe me."

Oh, Lord. Please, no more favors. "Sure."

"I was wondering if you could set me up with the caterer. You know? I think his name was Blake."

Sara thought for a moment, then shook

her head. "Honestly, I'm not a very good matchmaker. I think I'm finished with setting people up. But I'll be happy to give you his number."

Dakota smirked. "Whatever. I'll text you tomorrow."

Leah's voice came through Sara's headset. "We're ready for Dakota at the dolphin enclosure."

It was a hot August day, and even though sunset was nearing, it was still burning outside. Sara felt the heat penetrating the back of her blouse. Dakota didn't want anyone to see her before she came sailing in on the dolphins, so they hid behind several palm trees. From where they stood, Sara could see the other side of the dolphin enclosure. The crowd around the huge aquarium was massive.

She recognized lots of faces from school. Scantily clad, everyone had done a creative job of making their clothes look weathered. Most of the guys were topless, with ripped jeans and pants, shoes that were missing all the laces. The girls wore all kinds of torn, faded dresses and shirts with destroyed shorts. The only faces missing from the crowd were Allie's and Shane's. Though they'd both been invited, Allie said she couldn't bring herself to celebrate anything for Dakota.

All of Dakota's fans cheered and hollered for her. Someone in the crowd held a gigantic banner that read WE WANT DAKOTA BACK AT BAY SIDE! Tiki lamps burned and sexy rave music played from a set of speakers. Behind the crowd was the parking lot. She could see her mother waving down someone. She knew it was Dakota's father pulling up in her new convertible, trying to keep the car a secret.

The dolphin trainers came, and Sara decided it was a good time to leave Dakota. Sara wanted to find her own place to watch the grand entrance.

As she headed to the back of the crowd, she waved to Cassidy and a few other friends from the breakup party. She went to her usual position in the back and looked over some of the notes on her clipboard.

She felt an elbow in her ribs. Her first thought was Blake. But then she remembered he wasn't working here. She turned toward the elbow.

"Ian?" she said, even though she knew it was him. Maybe she just needed confirmation that she wasn't dreaming.

"Hey, Sara. I thought I'd find you here."

He was definitely real. It wasn't a dream, and she couldn't believe he was here. He'd come to Dakota's party? She wanted to throw her arms around his neck and pick up right where they'd left off that night at the beach.

Then it occurred to her. He wasn't here for her. He probably wanted his hoodie, or maybe he'd changed his mind and decided he wanted to be Dakota's date after all. Perhaps all the scandal that Dakota had been involved in could bring him publicity for the band. Her heart sank, but she maintained composure. "Hey, I still have your hoodie in my car."

"Cool, thanks."

She glanced at her watch. "I could take you there to get it right now. I have a few minutes."

He nodded. "All right."

They didn't say much as they walked to the parking lot. She unlocked her car door, slowly reached into the backseat, and pulled out the sweatshirt. She caught one final whiff of his clean, soapy scent.

She handed it over. For a moment they both stood there as if they were thinking of the best way to say good-bye.

"I just—"

"You know—"

"You first," he said.

"No, sorry. You first," she insisted. "Please, go ahead."

"I was just going to say that you must know I didn't come here for my sweatshirt."

"You didn't? I mean, I figured . . . did you want to come to the party?"

He smiled, then shook his head. "No. I came here because I wanted to talk to you in person, and I didn't want to—"

She couldn't help but interrupt. She'd felt like she had so much she wanted to say for so long. It had been bottled up, and now she had her chance to spill. "Ian, can I just say that I am so sorry? I am such an idiot, and I don't even deserve for you to come talk to me in person. I should've never said the things I did at the beach, and they weren't what I meant. I didn't ever want you to be Dakota's date. I just felt so pressured, and I know it's ridiculous now, but I—"

"It's okay. I know. I mean, I know you're sorry."

"What I should've said that night was that I like you. I've liked you from that first wedding when Mickey Piper almost kicked over the cake."

He smiled at the memory.

"But I was too wrapped up in making everyone else happy to stop and think about myself."

"Hey, look, I've done some stupid things too. It's only human."

"But not this stupid. Just hear me out for one second, because if I don't say all of this, I'll regret it forever. I just want you to know that I'm taking a little hiatus from the party planning. I'll still work for my mom a little bit, but I think I just want to make my own memories for the time being. I'm tired of focusing on other people's milestones. I hope we can at least be friends again."

He nodded. "I think at least."

"You don't hate me?"

He shook his head, then revealed his dimples. "I definitely don't hate you. My feelings couldn't be any more opposite than hating you.

"C'mere." He held out his hand to her.

Slowly, she took a step toward him. For a moment she looked at his face beneath the dim glow of dusk. She looked at the way his curls tumbled over his forehead and the way his blue eyes seemed to dance. She would never forget the way his fingertips felt on her chin when he gently tipped her face toward his, then softly brushed his lips over hers. His body was the warmest thing she'd ever felt as they moved into a snug embrace.

When they looked up, she could see Dakota gliding across the water, the dolphins propelling her with their long noses. She held her arms over her head, and her long hair flew up behind. After her dolphin ride, she swam to the edge of the pool and pulled herself from the water. She pointed in Sara's direction. Dakota's jaw dropped, and for a moment she thought Dakota was pointing at Ian and her. Then she noticed the convertible that Mr. London had just pulled to the front of the parking lot.

The funny thing was, Sara wasn't bitter about Dakota getting everything she wanted. Dakota had her car and her party. But Sara knew those things wouldn't make her happy for very long. As Sara looked at Ian, she felt like she'd gotten what mattered most.

Sara's headset crackled. "Sara, good-bye," her mother said.

"What?"

"I said good-bye. I'll see you later. I can handle the rest."

Sara looked up and saw her mother standing near the birthday crowd. Everyone went wild over Dakota's new car. Leah waved.

Sara ripped off her headset and looked at Ian.

"Let's get outta here," he said.

She took his hand. For the first time in her life, she felt like she had something worth celebrating.

About the Author

Whitney Lyles is the author of the novels *Always the Bridesmaid*, *Here Comes the Bride*, *First Comes Love*, and *Roommates*. She makes her YA debut with *Party Games*, and writing this book brought back many memories of her sixteenth birthday. Whitney admits she was grounded for the occasion—but still found a way to pass her driving test with flying colors.

Whitney lives with her husband and daughter in San Diego, California. Visit her on the Web at www.whitneylyles.com or www.myspace.com/whitney_lyles.

★

"Come on, you guys, *sit*. We have to wait until Curly pees." Alana Marks used a stern but calm voice to control three of her four charges, Nicolette, Frisky, and Noodles, as they waited for Curly to do her business near a bench in Central Park. "You've all had your turn. Now it's hers."

The bird-watchers standing nearby shot her an evil look. Alana sighed. She had a feeling they weren't too happy with her. The bird people never were. Not that she blamed them. After all, there was no chance any of the yellow-bellied sapsuckers or white-throated sparrows they were seeking would come near as long as there were four dogs around—especially four dogs who were as rambunctious as Nicolette, Frisky, Noodles, and Curly. Alana had been stand-ing there only a few seconds, and already Nicolette (the poodle) was growling angrily under her breath, Frisky (the Jack Russell terrier) was bouncing up and down like a jumping bean, and Noodles (the bulldog) was eyeing a mud puddle with far too much interest for Alana's taste.

She just didn't get it. Other dog walkers always seemed so in charge of their clients. But it seemed like her dogs were always out of control. Then again, maybe it wasn't that the *dogs* were out of control. Maybe it was just that *they* were controlling *her*. Either way, it was not a great position for a dog walker to be in.

Alana held tight to the four leashes and watched as Curly scratched at the gray dirt with her back paws and then looked up at her, ready to walk. Alana smiled. "Good girl," she complimented the golden-haired cocker spaniel. Curly raised her head proudly and glanced in the direction of the other dogs, as though she were making sure they'd heard her being praised. Alana giggled. Curly could be such a diva.

Alana had spent seventeen years—her whole life—in Manhattan, growing up not far from the park at Ninety-fifth and Columbus, but the Ramble section of Central Park never ceased to amaze her. The moment she stepped off the main road and into the wooded area, she felt as though she were in the woods. In fact, she often remarked that it "smelled like camp" in the Ramble, particularly right after it rained. It *felt* like a summer camp too—the thick trees, winding dirt paths, and babbling brooks were all like something you'd find in the Poconos or somewhere. In fact, if you didn't look up, you'd never know you were in New York City anymore. But the minute you did, there was no mistaking the huge skyscrapers that surrounded all of Central Park, towering over the haven like a giant concrete and glass fortress.

"Arooooo."

"Grrr!"

Alana was suddenly shaken from her thoughts by some wild jumping on the other end of the leashes. She looked in the dogs' direction and discovered the impetus for the sudden canine rebellion. A squirrel. A tiny little gray squirrel. Too small to do any damage to anyone. At least that's what you'd think if you weren't a dog walker. But Alana knew better. "Uh-oh," she murmured, fully aware of the effect squirrels had on the dogs.

For a moment all four dogs just stood there, watching. The squirrel stared back, afraid to move. Then, suddenly, it gathered the courage to make a run for it and scampered quickly in the direction of a nearby tree. . . .

Frisky was the first of the dogs to take action. He began bouncing up and down wildly, tugging on his leash in an attempt to run after the squirrel. Not to be outdone, Curly barked wildly and pulled at her leash, trying to get Alana to follow behind as she raced toward the thick tree at the end of the hill, to where the frightened gray squirrel had darted.

Nicolette, however, had spotted a second squirrel off to the right, and she was determined to get *that* one. Noodles didn't care which of the two squirrels he captured, as long as he got to chase something. As far as the bulldog was concerned, the majority ruled.

"WHOAAA!" Alana's voice echoed through the Ramble as the dogs took off in search of their prey. She could feel the leashes slipping from her grip as the dogs pulled her behind them, but she refused to let go. She was going to hold on to those dogs no matter what. Even if "no matter what" meant losing her footing and sliding headfirst on her stomach down a huge hill. "STOP!" Alana shouted as she slid downhill. "HEEL! NO! PLAY DEAD!" Any command, just to get them to stop.

And they did stop—with such a sudden force that Alana just missed slamming her head into a nearby tree. Still, she was pretty proud of herself. She'd finally gotten the dogs to obey her.

Or not. On closer inspection she discovered that the dogs had stopped only because they'd spotted a hot dog on the ground. At the moment, they were sharing the frankfurter and its accompanying bun with great glee. Alana knew that Mrs. Stanhope, Nicolette's owner, would be especially upset about the hot dog. Nicolette ate only gourmet dog food, bought at top price from the Barkery, an elite dog shop on Broadway. Actually, Nicolette did sometimes get people food— but even then the prized poodle was fed only the finest cuts of steak. Still, at the moment, Alana didn't care if Nicolette ate something as pedestrian as a dirty frankfurter. The poodle seemed happy enough.

And at least she was standing still. They all were.

But that wouldn't last long, and Alana knew it. Quickly the slender teen leaped to her feet and brushed her long, golden brown hair from her face. Looking down at her grass-stained white T-shirt and dark blue tight "skinny" jeans, she groaned. Darn it! Brand-new jeans, and now they had a huge hole in the knee. She'd probably torn them on a rock as she went down the hill—which would also explain the small trickle of blood coming from the cut on her knee. "Thanks so much, you guys," she grumbled sarcastically. But she couldn't stay angry with them for long. She never could. Alana had a real soft spot when it came to dogs. She adored them for their loyalty, their love, and their uncanny ability to know exactly when she needed a little canine comfort.

In fact, at just that moment, Curly, possibly sensing Alana's dismay, padded over to her and rubbed her soft furry body against Alana's calves. Then she looked up and gave her a smile. A genuine smile; the kind only a dog can pull off. And of course it melted Alana's heart. "I'm okay, Curly," she said gently as she pulled a leaf from her bangs.

Alana glanced around quickly. No one seemed to be around. That was something, anyway. Nobody had actually seen her free-fall down the grassy hill. She wasn't going to wind up in some amateur videographer's joke video on YouTube or anything. Thank goodness for small favors.

"Time to go home," Alana told the dogs as she began walking toward the exit of the park. For once, Nicolette, Curly, Noodles, and Frisky did as they were told, walking in unison toward Central Park West. It was as though their acute canine senses told them that they had gone too far this time and they'd better mind their manners. Alana was able to stroll toward the West Seventy-seventh Street exit of the park without incident.

As she reached the corner of Seventy-seventh and Central Park West, a big red double-decker tour bus pulled up. As it stopped at the red light, Alana could hear the tour guide's voice ringing out from the microphone. "And to your left is the American Museum of Natural History." Almost immediately the tourists on the top deck pulled out their cameras and began clicking away.

The odd thing was, the tourists were aiming their lenses to the right of the bus, not the left. They weren't shooting the huge stone museum; they were taking shots of Alana. For some reason they seemed to think that a grass-stained dog walker with ripped jeans, a bloody knee, and leaves in her hair was more interesting than the big statue of Teddy Roosevelt outside the museum. *Haven't these people ever seen a dog walker before?*

Apparently not, from the sound of the clicking cameras. Suddenly she'd become a tourist attraction! She could just see the guidebooks now—"Things you can't miss on your trip to New York: the Statue of Liberty, Ellis Island, the Empire State Building, and Alana Marks being pulled down the street by four wild and crazy dogs."

"Come on, you guys, let's move a little faster," Alana said as she urged the pups to walk up the block toward West Eighty-first Street. She waved at the tour bus as she and the dogs strolled by. "May as well give them a real show."

From **WILD** to **ROMANTIC**, don't miss these **PROM** stories from Simon Pulse!

A Really Nice Prom Mess

How I Created My
Perfect Prom Date

Prom Crashers

Prama

From Simon Pulse
* * *
Published by Simon & Schuster

Get smitten with these scrumptious British treats:

Prada Princesses
by Jasmine Oliver

Three friends tackle the high-stakes world of fashion school.

10 Ways to Cope with Boys
by Caroline Plaisted

What every girl *really* needs to know.

Does Snogging Count as Exercise?
by Helen Salter

For any girl who's tongue-tied around boys.

From Simon Pulse · Published by Simon & Schuster

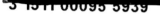